30 Ways To Dump A Sister

by Janet Adele Bloss
illustrated by Don Robison

To Mildred Foster,
my very first friend

Published by Willowisp Press, Inc.
401 E. Wilson Bridge Road, Worthington, Ohio 43085

Copyright ©1986 by Willowisp Press, Inc.

Printed in the United States of America

10 9 8 7 6 5 4

ISBN 0-87406-057-5

One

SHANDA Bates sat in the living room of her home reading a book. It was a Saturday afternoon in October. It seemed a little too chilly to be playing outside. Shanda's attention was interrupted as she looked out the picture window. A boy in a blue jacket was slowly pedaling his bike past her house on Willowby Street. She put down her book and watched the boy's tall, slender form. He leaned over the handlebars and glided down the road. She smiled to herself when he turned his bike around. He slowly pedaled by her house again, then again. All in all, Shanda counted six times. The boy turned his bike around and rode by her house as if he couldn't make up his mind where he was going. At last, he guided his bike into the Bates' driveway and hopped off. Shanda felt her heart begin to beat faster as she slid her book under the couch. She waited for whatever was to happen next.

The doorbell rang and eleven-year-old Shanda Bates hurried to answer it. She took a quick look at her reflection in the hall mirror as she passed. Bright blue eyes stared back at her from a face framed by golden blonde curls. Shanda opened the door and there stood Paul Seckler. He was in Shanda's sixth grade class at Grayson Elementary School. His bicycle lay in the browning autumn grass of Shanda's front yard.

"Hi, Shanda," Paul said. "I was riding my bike in your neighborhood and I thought I'd stop in and see if you were home. Can I come in?" Puffs of vapor came from Paul's mouth with each word. "Whew!" he exclaimed with a laugh. "It's cold out here!"

Shanda opened the door wider. "Come on in," she said.

"Your parents won't mind, will they?" asked

Paul, taking off his jacket.

"No," Shanda reassured him. "Mom's not home, anyway. Even though it's Saturday, she had to go to work. She works for a perfume company and she's working on some new account. Dad's out in the kitchen as usual."

Shanda sighed. Sometimes it was hard to explain that her father didn't have a regular job like most fathers. Her dad worked for different magazines and publishers, writing cookbooks. He didn't have an office to drive to every morning. He wore an apron instead of a suit. He spent his time working in the kitchen at home. He combined strange ingredients and concocted creative, tasty dishes to try out on his family. The kids at school looked at Shanda strangely when she told them that her father was a cook. Once "Dirt" Darby, a boy in Shanda's class, had said, "That's a weird job for a man to have. I thought only moms were supposed to bake. What does your mother do? Drive a truck?" Shanda hadn't laughed. She was tired of the jokes some people made about her father.

"What's your dad doing in the kitchen?" asked Paul, following Shanda into the living room.

Shanda held her breath as she said, "He's baking a triple-fudge angel cake. Last time it turned out pretty bad. He's going to try it with extra eggs and a little cinnamon this time. It's for a dessert cookbook that he's writing. Desserts are his specialty." Shanda searched Paul's eyes for his reaction to this bit of information.

"Neat," said Paul. "I love anything with chocolate in it. About the only thing my dad can make is scrambled eggs. I can make a pretty good bowl of buttered popcorn, even if I do say so myself." Paul smiled.

Shanda sighed with relief. Her shoulders relaxed. "Sit down," she said. From the kitchen came the sound of pots and pans rattling. A man's voice hummed contentedly. "Do you want to listen to some music?" asked Shanda, hoping Paul would like the idea. "I have the new Robots album. Well, it's not really new," she said apologetically. "But it's the newest one I have."

"Sure," said Paul. "That sounds great."

Shanda went to the corner of the living room toward the stereo. A shelf of albums stretched beside the stereo speakers. She pulled a black-jacketed album from a pile on the floor. She placed the record carefully on the turntable. Cheerful singing and rhythmic guitar playing filled the room. Outside, a chilly wind railed aimlessly at the large living room window. Shanda returned to her cushioned seat next to Paul on the couch.

"I'm really glad you were home," said Paul, smiling shyly. "I wanted to ask you something in class the other day, but I never got the chance."

Suddenly a metallic crash resounded from the kitchen. It sounded as if every cake and pie tin that the Bates owned had been hurled onto the linoleum floor. Shanda and Paul jumped to their feet at the sound of the crash. "Darn it!" yelled a man's voice. "Butter!" he shouted. "I thought I told you to stay off the counters! If you want a glass, you should ask your sister for it! She'll get it for you. I'm up to my elbows in fudge and I can't watch you right now! Okay, honey?" he said, dropping his voice to a calmer tone.

Shanda and Paul looked toward the kitchen as its swinging door pushed open. A man's head poked out. He wore metal wire-rimmed glasses perched atop a large nose. Beneath his nose was a thick, droopy moustache. "Oh, hi there," Karl Bates said, as he saw Paul. "I didn't know we had company," he said. A friendly grin stretched across his face.

"This is a friend from school," explained Shanda. "Paul, this is my dad."

"Glad to meet you, Mr. Bates," said Paul.

Shanda's father strode into the room with his arm outstretched. A fudge-streaked apron was wrapped around Mr. Bates' lean body. He shook Paul's hand and said, "Sorry for all the commotion in the kitchen. I'm afraid Shanda's little sister is doing gymnastics on the counters again. That always spells disaster." As if on cue, the kitchen door swung open and the youngest member of the Bates family came skipping out.

Shanda turned apologetic eyes to Paul saying, "This is my sister, Butter."

"Butter?" asked Paul.

The little six-year-old girl stood in front of Paul. She stared at him from under a blonde pixie haircut. She wore baggy green pants with brown patches sewn over the knees. Suddenly a grin lit up her face, showing a space where two front teeth used to be. Butter stood silently, staring and grinning at Paul.

"I've got to get back to my cake," said Mr. Bates. "Nice to meet you, Paul," he said. "Why don't you hang around for a while. You can be one of my guinea pigs and test the cake when it comes out of the oven."

"Sure," said Paul. "It smells great." The scent of warm chocolate was beginning to fill the air.

"Shanda, keep an eye on Butter for a while, all right?" asked Shanda's father. "I want this cake to turn out right." He turned and hurried back through the swinging door into the kitchen.

Paul looked down at the scrappy little girl who stood staring before him. "So, your name's Butter?" he asked her.

"Yes," she said, lisping slightly. "Butter Marie Bates." She pointed to the gap where her two front teeth used to be. "Look! My teeth fell out. I got two quarters from the tooth fairy. I put my teeth under my pillow and she came while I was sleeping. I love the tooth fairy!"

Shanda rolled her eyes impatiently. "Her name's really Bethany. But when she was little Dad started calling her 'Butter.' One night Dad and Mom came in to check on her while she was sleeping. Dad thought her blonde hair on the white pillow looked like a pat of butter. He probably thought that because he's a cook. Anyway, that's how she got the nickname 'Butter.'"

Shanda and Paul walked back to the couch and sat down. Butter followed them, still staring at Paul. She held a chubby little hand out to him

and said, "Look! There's a booger on my finger."
She smiled and showed it to Paul as if it were
something very special.

"Oh, gross!" yelled Shanda. She pushed her
sister's arm away and glanced at Paul. She was
pleased to see that he was laughing quietly.
Butter looked surprised at the reaction that her
outstretched finger had brought. She wiped her
hand against her pants. She sniffled her nose at
the same time.

"I told you *my* name. Now you tell me *yours,*"
said Butter, ignoring Shanda. She stood with her
hands shoved into the pockets of her green play
pants.

"Fair enough," said Paul. "I'm Paul Seckler.
I'm in your sister's class at school."

"Do you go to Grayson Elementary?" asked
Butter, grinning.

"Yeah," said Paul.

"So do I," Butter informed him importantly.
"I'm in the first grade. Mrs. Bryant is my
teacher."

11

"I had her in first grade, too," said Paul.

Shanda rose from the couch and walked to the stereo. She flipped over the record. As she adjusted the volume, she heard Butter's voice behind her.

"I know a secret," said Butter confidentially.

Paul's voice sounded encouraging as he said, "Oh, really?"

"Yes," said Butter. "I know a secret and it's about YOU!"

Shanda stood up quickly at this new bit of information. She glanced nervously at Butter. "Why don't you go play in your room?" she suggested. "Paul doesn't want to hear any of your baby secrets."

Butter stood immovable in the center of the room, facing Paul. She grinned mischievously. "I listened to Shanda talking on the phone to Pam last night," she said. "I listened to everything they said and they were talking about YOU!"

"Oh, really?" Paul shifted uncomfortably in his seat, looking curiously at Butter.

12

Shanda reached out and grabbed Butter by the hand. She pulled her over to the foot of the stairs. "Don't you have some homework to do?" she asked.

"Nope," Butter replied.

"Well, then you'd better go clean your room. Okay? Please?" begged Shanda.

Butter climbed the stairs slowly as Shanda walked back toward Paul. Then Butter crouched down and stuck her head between the railings. She yelled at the top of her lungs, "Shanda's in love with Paul! Shanda's in love with Paul!" Butter began laughing wildly as Shanda whirled around glaring at her. "I heard Shanda tell Pam that you're the cutest hunk in the whole school! Shanda wants to be your girl friend!"

Shanda stared at Butter's little blonde head peeking through the railings. It looked to Shanda as if Butter were behind bars. Shanda's mind began to drift.

The sign by the zoo cage said MONKEYS—DO NOT FEED! Shanda approached the cage and

peered in. With a gasp, she saw that her own little sister was hanging onto the bars of the cage. On either side of Butter two monkeys sat. Occasionally the monkeys scratched themselves with long, hairy arms. Shanda walked nearer to the cage, staring in disbelief. Butter and her monkey friends laughed and pointed at her. Suddenly embarrassed, Shanda hurried past the cage.

Shanda shook the daydream from her head. She ran toward the bottom of the stairs. Butter scurried up the steps and down the hall. The sound of a bedroom door slamming echoed into the living room. Shanda turned around to see Paul sitting nervously on the edge of the couch. A strange smile twitched at the corner of his lips as he stared down at the floor.

Shanda rolled her eyes. "You know how little sisters are, don't you? Sometimes they make up stories. They have great imaginations," she said.

Shanda didn't sit on the couch beside Paul this time. She sat primly in a chair on the other side of the room. She hoped that Paul couldn't see that she was telling a white lie. Butter had been telling the truth when she said that Shanda and Pam were talking about Paul on the telephone. And what's more, Shanda really had said that Paul Seckler was the cutest hunk in the whole school and that she wanted to be his girl friend.

"My little sister has a wild imagination," she said again. She tried to make her voice sound firm and convincing. "I don't know where she got that story." Shanda forced a laugh, but it sounded a little shaky. She gently patted her blonde curls and tried to think of a good way to change the subject. But nothing came to her mind.

Paul pushed his slim body up from the couch. He nervously cleared his throat. His eyes darted around the room. "Where's my jacket?" he asked. "I really should be going now. It's getting kind of late. I told my dad I'd be home in time to watch the Steelers' game with him on TV."

"You can watch it here if you want to," suggested Shanda. "We have a TV, too." She could have kicked herself for saying such a stupid thing. EVERYBODY has a TV, she reminded herself. "I mean, you can watch the game here. I really like football a lot," she said, telling her second white lie of the day. Shanda really thought that football was a boring game. But the thought of sitting beside Paul suddenly gave football a new attraction.

"Sorry," said Paul, pulling on his jacket. He stuffed his hands into leather gloves. "I promised my dad I'd watch the game with him." Paul walked to the front door with Shanda following behind him. "Say good-bye to your dad and Butter for me, okay?" he said.

"Okay. Bye," Shanda's voice called softly. She watched from the door as Paul walked down the steps. He climbed on his bicycle and disappeared down Willowby Street. A gust of cold wind reminded Shanda of the bone-chilling October weather outside. She quickly closed the door and returned to the living room. She sat alone on the couch thinking of how her little sister had ruined

Paul's visit. She remembered the worst moment when Butter told Paul that Shanda wanted to be his girl friend. How embarrassing! Shanda thought about Butter kneeling beside the stair railings. She really had looked like a zoo animal in a cage. Oh, Shanda thought, if only she really were in a zoo! That would be the perfect place for a little sister like Butter.

It made such a crazy picture in Shanda's mind that she had to laugh. She reached for her school notebook on the coffee table and grabbed a pencil. She began to sketch a picture of her sister, standing in a cage, surrounded by little monkeys.

Shanda thought, Maybe if I write down some ideas on how to get rid of Butter, I can sell them to a magazine. Other people might be interested in how to dump their little sisters. Maybe I can help other older sisters by keeping this list.

Shanda chewed on her pencil's eraser for a moment before writing at the top of the page.

Ways to Dump a Sister

1 Take her to the zoo and let her live
with the monkeys.

Shanda thought for a moment. Then she added:

2 Take your sister to the fun house at
the park. Leave her in the "crazy-door
room." That will keep her busy for a
long time.

The kitchen door swung open and Shanda's
father walked in to the living room. He carried a
fudgey-looking cake on a platter. Swirls of steam
rose from chocolate goo that dripped down the
sides of the cake. "I think I've done it this time,"
said Mr. Bates excitedly. He placed the platter
on the coffee table. "Where's Paul?" he asked,
looking around. "I was hoping he'd like a sample.
I think the extra eggs did the trick," he added
proudly.

"Paul had to leave," said Shanda. She folded
the list she'd begun and slid it into her jean's

pocket. Her list was meant to be seen by older sisters and not by parents.

"Butter!" called Mr. Bates. "The cake's ready!" A door was thrown open. Little sneakers squeaked furiously across the upstairs floor and down the stairs. Shanda glared as Butter stretched her hands out for a piece of cake. But Butter smiled and licked her lips. She looked at Shanda as if nothing at all had happened. Shanda frowned as she remembered how Butter had embarrassed her—in front of a boy. And it was not just *any* boy, but *the* boy of Shanda's daydreams. It was not just on *any* day, but on the *first* day that he had ever come to visit.

Shanda took a bite of cake. It was warm, chocolaty, and creamy. It melted on her tongue. "M-m-m-m-m," she said approvingly, looking at her father. "This is really great, Dad," she said. "I think you've got a winner here."

Mr. Bates nodded, beaming happily.

Butter gobbled down her cake and licked her plate. "Yummy!" she shrieked. Mr. Bates leaned over and kissed Butter on top of her head.

Shanda rolled her eyes in exasperation. She thought about the folded list in her pocket. She would need to add:

3 Give your sister to a relative who lives
in another state.

I could give Butter to Aunt Margaret in Denver, Shanda thought. I could give Aunt Margaret the $26.58 I saved. Maybe she'll think she's not getting such a bad deal. Maybe she'll think Butter's really a sweet kid.

Mr. Bates took the dirty plates back to the kitchen. Shanda was left with Butter in the living room.

"Did your boyfriend leave?" asked Butter innocently. "Doesn't he like you anymore?"

Shanda pulled her list from her pocket and unfolded it. She began to write.

4 Find your little sister a boyfriend of
her own. Then maybe she'll leave you

alone when *your* boyfriend comes over.
But you'll probably have to go to
another planet to find one for her.

"Do you think I'm prettier than you?" asked
Butter. She smiled and Shanda stared at the gap
where her sister's teeth used to be. Shanda
sighed, wondering how Butter thought of such
crazy questions. Shanda picked up her pen.

5 Get your sister to eat a whole fudge
angel cake. Maybe then she'll act like
an angel instead of a pest.

"Why don't you go to the kitchen," said Shanda.
"I'll bet Dad would let you eat some more cake."
Butter poked a brown chocolate-coated tongue
at her older sister. "I'm prettier than you!" she
squealed, pointing a finger at her older sister.
Shanda grit her teeth together and bent over
her paper. She wrote:

6 Glue your sister's lips together so she
can't stick her tongue out at you.

Shanda leaned back into the couch's soft cushions and smiled to herself. If she thought of enough ideas maybe, just maybe, one of them would work. There *had* to be a way to teach a little sister to act like a regular person.

Shanda's thoughts drifted to more pleasant subjects. She remembered the tall, slim boy who'd ridden his bicycle through the cold October weather to visit her.

Butter looked impishly at Shanda who was lost in her private world of thoughts. Butter's tongue darted out at a speck of chocolate lodged in the corner of her mouth. "I'm going to live in a tree house when I get married," Butter said suddenly. "You can come and visit me if you want to. And I'll let you ride my bicycle and use my telephone."

"Gee, thanks," sighed Shanda.

Two

"MOM, do I have to walk with Butter to school today?" asked Shanda over her bowl of cereal. "Isn't Butter old enough to walk by herself? The school's only a few blocks away and it's just a ten-minute walk. I'm tired of having her tag along with me all the time."

Marge Bates sat at the breakfast table in a navy blue suit. She held a cup of coffee in one hand and a piece of toast in the other. "Sorry, honey," she said. "Butter's too little to walk alone. In just another year or two she'll be old enough to walk by herself. But for now I'd feel better if you were with her."

"I'm going to walk with you every day forever 'cause you're my friend!" announced Butter with a mouthful of cereal. A stream of milk dribbled through the gap where her two front teeth used to be, splashing onto the table.

"Gross!" yelled Shanda. She looked at her mother. "Can you at least teach her how to eat properly?" she asked. "She eats like a pig. It's embarrassing."

"Oink! Oink!" Butter snorted. She pushed the tip of her nose up with her finger. Squashed against the bridge of her nose, her nostrils appeared round and piglike. "Oink! Oink!" she said again. Mrs. Bates laughed.

Shanda heaved a heavy sigh.

"Oh, come on, Shanda," said Mrs. Bates. "Don't take it so seriously. Butter's only six years old."

"Am not!" announced Butter. "I'm ninety-eight-forty-hundred-zillion!"

"That's pretty old," said Mrs. Bates laughingly.

"I'm beginning to feel that old," said Shanda.

The kitchen door swung open and Mr. Bates walked in. He smiled as he wrapped an apron around his waist. Shanda returned her dad's smile and ate her last bite of cereal.

"Hey!" exclaimed Mr. Bates. "You guys are running late this morning," he said, glancing at his watch. "I've got a poppy seed almond roll to make today and it takes hours for the bread to rise. I've got to get started and I'll need that table."

"Okay, okay," said Mrs. Bates, smiling. She rose from the table and put on her coat. "I've got a conference to go to this morning," she said. "We're planning a new perfume. I've been thinking of calling it 'Meadow Mist.' Do you like that name?"

"Sounds nice," said Mr. Bates.

"I like it, too, Mom," said Shanda. "It's a pretty name."

"I do, too," said Mrs. Bates. "Anyway," she said, turning to face her family, "I've got to go. Bye." She swiftly kissed Shanda, Butter, then her husband. Mr. Bates held her in his arms for a moment and said, "Have a nice day, Sugar. Go get 'em!" He kissed her again.

Mrs. Bates picked up her briefcase and left through the swinging door. Shanda heard the front door close. A car engine roared in the driveway, then faded down Willowby Street.

Shanda stood by the refrigerator, buttoning up her coat. She impatiently tapped her foot. "Come on, Butter," she said. "You're going to make us late for school again."

"No I won't!" shouted Butter with glee. "I'm the fastest coat-putter-onner in the world!" She jumped up from the table. She raced through the kitchen door in a wink of an eye. The door swung back violently, hitting Shanda's shoulder.

"Ow!" yelled Shanda. She looked at her father for sympathy. "Dad," she moaned. "Can't you do something about Butter? She's slow when she should be fast and fast when she should be slow. It seems like she does *everything* backward. Can't you make her be like a regular person with a brain that works?"

"I'm picking up some negative vibrations

here," her father said gently. He patted Shanda's shoulder and looked directly into her eyes. Shanda felt the smile behind her father's twinkling eyes. In spite of herself, she smiled back.

Her father always talked about positive and negative vibrations. He said vibrations were electrical currents that moved from one person's heart to another's. He said that good thoughts make good vibrations that fly out into the air and make the world a nicer place to live in.

The kitchen door swung wildly again, knocking Shanda's books from her hands onto the floor. "Slow down!" ordered Shanda. Butter stood grinning with the wide gap in her front teeth.

"You told me to hurry," Butter informed Shanda.

Shanda rolled her eyes toward the ceiling. "Bye, Dad," Shanda said, kissing her father on his moustache.

"Bye, sweetheart," he said. Mr. Bates bent and kissed Butter on the tip of her nose. "I'm sending some good vibrations with you," he said. "I'm sending some with you, too, Shanda," he informed her, waving a hand in her direction.

"Thanks, Dad," said Shanda with an understanding look. "Come on, Butter." Shanda grabbed Butter's hand and pushed through the kitchen door. They walked rapidly through the living room and out the front door. Outside, a frosty wind caused the sisters to shove their mittened hands deep into their pockets. A few brown leaves skipped beside them as they hurried down Willowby Street. They walked past some small houses. Most of these houses were painted in pastel shades of blue, pink, and green. Their own house was yellow. It's the same color as butter, Shanda thought with a frown. There was no way for her to escape the constant reminder that she had a pesty six-year-old sister.

The five-minute bell rang just as Shanda and Butter hurried breathlessly through the school's front doors. Two of Shanda's best friends, Pam and Susan, went rushing by. "Better hurry!"

called Pam. "You know how Mrs. Blandon is about being late to class."

"Really," agreed Susan, looking over her shoulder at Shanda. "She'll make you stay after class if you're late. I had to stay twice last week. Boring!"

"Bye!" Butter yelled. She rushed off to her class.

Shanda stood for a moment watching the students running through the hall. Then she joined the flow of girls and boys and was carried along to her class. She took her seat just as the last bell rang. Mrs. Blandon stood at the front of the class looking grimly back at the students. Shanda looked at the teacher's down-turned mouth and hollow cheeks.

"Negative vibrations," she muttered under her breath.

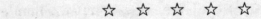

Her math class was studying fractions. Shanda

thought it was interesting. The great thing about math problems is that they all have answers, Shanda thought. You can depend on numbers to make sense. Too bad little sisters can't be more like math problems. Shanda frowned. There's no answer to the problems of how to live with a tag-a-long sister. Why can't younger sisters be as easy as $\frac{3}{4} \times \frac{1}{2} = \frac{3}{8}$?

Shanda solved the math problems on the blackboard. She spent the rest of the time staring at the back of Paul Seckler's head. He sat two rows up and one row over. Shanda couldn't tell if he was ignoring her or if he was just being his usual self. He rarely said anything to her in math class anyway.

Shanda jumped up from her desk at the sound of the lunch bell and joined the throng of students hurrying toward the cafeteria.

She took a tray. One of the school's cooks handed her a plate of watery spaghetti. Shanda spotted Pam and Susan at a table by a window. She wriggled her way through the crowd. "Hi," she said, setting her tray down and lowering herself into a chair. "How's it going?"

"Fine, I guess," exclaimed Pam. "I sure wish that Ronnie Arps would notice me. I'm beginning to think I'm invisible. I'm not, am I?" she asked, holding her arms out in front of her face.

"Hi, everyone," said Gloria Finley, placing her tray beside Pam's. "Was everyone as bored in math class this morning as I was?" The brown-haired, freckled girl turned to look at Shanda. "Has your dad baked any cute little cakes lately?" she asked, giggling.

Shanda chewed her watery spaghetti without saying a word to Gloria.

"Hi! Can I sit with you guys?"

Shanda froze at the sound of the voice. She turned to stare into a pixie face. "Hi, Butter," she said. "What's wrong? Why aren't you with your friends?"

"I want to sit with *you*," announced Butter with a slight lisp. She shoved her tray beside Shanda's and sat down. Her face cleared the top of the table by only a few inches. She pursed her lips around the straw in her chocolate milk carton. *Slurp! Slurp! Slurp!* Shanda became aware of everyone around the table, turning to stare at her little sister. *Slurp!* Butter sucked at the straw and smiled at the same time. Her smile revealed a stretch of pink upper gum. Shanda continued to eat her spaghetti, pretending that the seat beside her was still empty.

"My stereo broke last night," announced Pam with a frown. "I think I blew out the speakers. It's a real drag, because I just got a new album. I only got to hear it once."

"Bring your album over tomorrow after school," said Shanda. "My stereo's working." She looked around the table at the faces of Pam, Susan, and Gloria. "Why don't you all come over tomorrow after school?" she suggested. "I'll ask my dad if you can come for dinner. My dad always likes it when he has new guinea pigs. How about it?"

"Sounds good to me," said Pam. "It's pork

chop night at our house. My mom always cooks them until they taste like rubber."

"Sure, I'll ask my mom," said Susan. "I love your dad's desserts!"

"Me, too," said Gloria. "I'm sure my mom will say it's okay. You know, your dad must be really weird to do all your cooking. It's usually the mother that does the cooking."

"Your nose is big," said Butter suddenly. She looked curiously into Gloria's face. "It looks like a pink pickle."

Gloria stiffly sat up. She pulled her face away from Butter who was leaning halfway across the table. Around the table mouths struggled to hold back smiles. Gloria lowered her chin, trying to hide her nose from public viewing.

Shanda hurried to change the subject. "What's that spot on your blouse, Butter?" she asked. "Look at you! You're a mess!"

Butter smiled happily. "We finger painted in class today. I put paint all over my paper!" She swept her arms through the air, showing her painting technique. Her arm knocked into her carton of chocolate milk. It tumbled over and splashed onto Pam and Gloria. A brown stain spread across Pam's white blouse. Everyone at the table jumped to their feet, shrieking. They pushed away from the little dribbles of brown milk that fell from the table's edge.

"Butter!" yelled Shanda. She grabbed some napkins and began sopping up the mess. Pam and Susan brought tissues from their purses and patted the stains on their blouses.

"Look at my skirt!" wailed Gloria. "This is a new skirt! It was super expensive, too."

"She didn't mean to do it," said Shanda. "Gee. I'm really sorry."

Pam looked at the large brown stain across her chest. "Remind me not to sit across from Butter tomorrow at your house," she said.

"I'm really sorry," Shanda said again. "I'll help you wash it out if you want me to."

Butter sat quietly in her chair as the older girls straightened the table. Then they sat down and

looked at the milk-soaked remains of their lunch. Shanda saw that Butter's chin was beginning to tremble. That was a sure sign that Butter would soon be crying. "It's okay, Butter," Shanda hurried to say. "Don't worry. It'll wash out." Butter's chin stopped trembling. Shanda thought, Butter is always embarrassing me in front of my friends. Her mind wandered.

A sea of chocolate milk flowed through Grayson Elementary School. It carried an empty milk carton. On top of the carton sat Butter who was no bigger than a thumb. She wore a tiny sailor cap and white bell-bottoms. Butter was using straws for oars. She was rowing her milk-carton boat far, far away.

"I can't believe this spot on my skirt!" Gloria continued to wail. "It'll cost a fortune to have it cleaned!"

Shanda took the list from her purse and quickly wrote:

7 Let your sister live with someone like

Gloria for two years. Be sure they have to share the same room.

Shanda twirled strands of dripping brown spaghetti from her fork. It really isn't too bad, she thought. She chewed it and thought of a cooking suggestion for her father. Perhaps he could put chocolate into his spaghetti sauce.

Staring at her lunch, Shanda imagined Butter lost in a forest of spaghetti.

Spaghetti was everywhere—hanging from trees, drooping over bushes, and sprouting straight up from the ground. Even the birds' nests were woven out of spaghetti.

Shanda picked up her pen and wrote:

8 Lose your sister in a dense forest of watery spaghetti.

Suddenly, the sound of sobbing erupted from beside Shanda. She quickly turned to see Butter's shoulders shaking. Tears streamed down her cheeks and fell onto her blue overalls. Heads from surrounding tables turned to stare as Butter's sobs grew louder.

"This is so embarrassing!" hissed Gloria.

"What's the matter, Butter?" asked Shanda.

"I spilled my chocolate milk," said Butter.

Shanda smiled wryly and said, "Yes, I know."

"I want some more," whined Butter. "I want some chocolate milk."

"Lunch is almost over," said Shanda. "You won't have time to drink it."

"I need a quarter," said Butter. "I want some milk, but I don't have any money."

"No," said Shanda. "You've caused enough trouble for one day."

Butter's voice grew louder. "I want some milk!" she cried. "I want some chocolate milk!"

"Give the poor kid a carton of milk!" came a voice from somewhere in the cafeteria. A quarter came sailing through the air and landed in Shanda's spaghetti. Butter grabbed it, taking a few strings of spaghetti with it. She pushed her chair away from the table. She ran to the milk case as the cafeteria erupted in laughter.

Shanda pushed her plate away from herself. She picked up her pen and began writing.

"Since when did you become the great writer?" asked Gloria. Shanda didn't say a word. Instead she added number nine to the list. She wrote:

9 Bribe your sister with a quarter. Make her promise never to eat lunch with you again.

Just as the bell rang, Butter hurried back to the table. She tipped the milk carton up to her mouth. Gulping as fast as she could, she finished drinking. Then she slipped her hand into Shanda's. Shanda glanced down at her sister. She saw that Butter's upper lip was covered by a large chocolate "moustache."

Shanda and Butter joined the crowd of students pushing their way out of the cafeteria. Shanda looked at all the different faces and heads around her. She wondered who had tossed the quarter into her spaghetti.

Three

"DINNER'S almost ready," said Karl Bates. "When are all your friends arriving?"

"Any minute, Dad," said Shanda. "Pam, Susan, and Gloria are real excited about trying your new dessert. I hope it's something good."

The front door opened and in walked Marge Bates. She put her briefcase on the floor. "Whew!" she said, heaving a big sigh. "What a day! We had a terrific meeting this morning. Everyone loved the name 'Misty Meadows.'"

"Good deal, Mom!" cried Shanda.

"Congratulations!" said Mr. Bates. He grabbed his wife and waltzed her around the room. They laughed and looked happily into each other's

41

eyes. Shanda thought about what neat parents she had. She liked the fact that her mother was a consultant for a perfume company. And her father was doing what he liked to do: working at home in the kitchen.

"Yes," Shanda sighed to herself. "It would be the perfect family if only my parents had one child instead of two. They should've stopped after I was born."

The doorbell rang. Shanda hurried to let her three friends into the house. "Hi, Mr. Bates," said Pam, pulling a knit cap from her head. "What's for dessert tonight?"

"How does peach ice cream on homemade angel food cake sound?" he asked. "We're having roast leg of lamb with raisin sauce tonight. And I've got a poppy seed almond roll that will melt in your mouth!"

"Yum!" exclaimed Pam. "That sounds great!"

"Hi, Pam," said Butter, running into the room. "Hi, Susan." She looked at Gloria and said, "You're the girl with the funny nose."

"Darn it, Butter!" exclaimed Shanda. "If you mention noses one more time, I'm going to punch *yours!*"

"Oh, wow," said Mr. Bates. "I feel negative vibrations. Come on, Shanda. Pull yourself together." He straightened his apron and said, "I've got a few more things to do out in the kitchen. Dinner will be served in about fifteen minutes."

"I'll help you, honey, as soon as I change clothes," said Marge Bates. "Hi, girls," she said with a smile. "Make yourselves at home." Then she turned and went upstairs to change.

"I brought my new Bash-Bang album," said Pam. "Do you want to listen to it now or after dinner?"

"Let's hear it now," said Shanda. "Everyone's talking about how great it is. We can go up to my room."

"Can I come?" asked Butter.

"No," said Shanda. "You'll just get in the way. You always do."

"Aw, let her come," said Susan. "She's not so bad."

"Yeah. I think your sister's cute," said Pam. "Let her hear the record, too."

"Okay," said Shanda hesitantly. "You can come. Just promise to be good, okay?"

"I promise," said Butter solemnly.

The four friends and Butter climbed the stairs to Shanda's room. Shanda took the Bash-Bang album from Pam and placed it on her turntable. She turned up the volume as music poured from the speakers. Butter exclaimed, "I like it!" Shanda watched as Butter began to dance.

Butter wiggled her fingers and hopped like a bunny. Susan began to giggle. She whispered, "Your sister looks like she learned how to dance on a pogo stick."

All eyes were turned to Butter as she wiggled and jumped. Shanda imagined idea number ten for her list.

The floor beneath Butter opened up. Butter's hopping stopped as she disappeared through a trap door and slid down a long slide—down, down until she came out somewhere—anywhere but in Shanda's bedroom.

"Butter, stop it!" pleaded Shanda. "You'll make the record skip."

"I love this music," said Butter, still hopping. "I'm the best dancer in the world! Want me to do a cartwheel?"

"No," said Shanda with a frown.

"I bet if I keep jumping I can learn to fly," said Butter. "Wouldn't that be neat?"

The idea of flying made Shanda think of number eleven for her *Ways to Dump a Sister* list.

If Butter could fly then I could open my bedroom window. She could fly through it—up and away. She could fly south for the winter and live in a tree with a family of birds. Shanda smiled to herself. *Probably cuckoo birds would be the best family for Butter to join.*

At last Butter grew tired of hopping. But she still had enough energy left to skip around

Shanda's room. She sang along loudly with the Bash-Bang album, even though she didn't know the words or the tune. Gloria clapped her hands over her ears. She looked at Shanda as if she thought Shanda's little sister were very strange indeed. "Can't you get rid of her?" whispered Gloria. Pam giggled.

"You wouldn't think she was so funny if you had to live with her," moaned Shanda. "I'm serious. Sometimes she drives me nuts."

Shanda wondered what the best way would be to get Butter to leave her room. At last she said, "Butter, you'd better leave now before you get sick."

"I feel okay," said Butter, breathing heavily. She stopped her skipping and stared questioningly into her older sister's eyes. "I don't feel sick at all," she said.

"Maybe you don't *now*. But you *will*," Shanda warned. "Don't you know that when kids in the first grade jump around too much, their tonsils fall out? It's true. I've seen it happen."

"Really?" asked Butter suspiciously. "What're tonsils?"

"They're something on the inside of your neck. They fall out when you hop and skip to Rock 'n Roll music," said Shanda with a serious face.

Pam began to giggle. Then she covered her mouth with her hand. Susan and Gloria snorted, holding back their laughter.

"I don't feel so well," said Butter suddenly. "I hope my tonsils aren't falling out. Do you think they are?"

"They might be," said Shanda. "You'd better go downstairs and rest. I wouldn't want you to get sick."

"Yeah," said Gloria. "It could be too late. You'd better leave."

"Promise you're not making this up?" asked Butter.

"I promise," said Shanda. "Right, girls?" She looked around at her friends for support.

"That's right," they all said.

"First graders shouldn't jump and listen to

music at the same time," said Susan. "It's really dangerous."

"Oooo," groaned Butter. "I don't feel very well. I'd better go lie down." She walked very slowly to the door. Her fingers gingerly searched her neck for signs of the mysterious tonsils. As soon as the door closed behind her, the four sixth graders shook with laughter.

"I can't believe she fell for it!" Susan said with a giggle. "Really, Shanda, I wish I had a little sister to play tricks on."

Shanda just rolled her eyes. She giggled, thinking of Butter resting downstairs, trying to keep her tonsils from falling out. Only a six-year-old sister would fall for such a story, she thought smugly.

From the ground floor Shanda heard her father call, "Dinner is served! Come and get it!"

Shanda led her friends down the stairs and into the dining room. They were still giggling. Butter sat, pale faced, at the table.

"Wow, Dad," exclaimed Shanda. "The table

looks great! Candles and everything!"

"The candles were my idea," said her mother.

"That's right," laughed her father. "Don't underestimate your mother's love of romance. I remember back when we first got married we ate by candlelight every night for almost a year." He winked and grinned at his wife.

"Oh, Karl," said Mrs. Bates shyly.

Shanda was glad that she had the kind of parents who loved each other and weren't embarrassed to show it. But sometimes, Shanda thought, it's embarrassing in front of my friends. "Pass the milk, please," said Shanda.

"Mmmm!" exclaimed Pam with a mouthful of almond poppy seed roll. "I don't think I've ever had this before!"

Shanda cut a steaming piece of lamb. She sniffed at the lamb, then popped it into her mouth. "Mmmm! This is great, Dad," she said. Voices agreed from around the table. But Butter said nothing. She stared sadly at her plate.

Shanda breathed a sigh of relief. She thought

to herself, dinner is great. Maybe Gloria will see how neat it is to have a dad who can cook like a great chef.

"May I have another piece of that almond poppy seed roll?" asked Gloria.

"Sure you can," said Mr. Bates, beaming. "You know, that's my very own recipe. I'm putting it into a bread cookbook that I'm writing. It might be sweet enough to put into my dessert cookbook."

"What's the matter, honey? Aren't you feeling well?" Marge Bates leaned over and felt Butter's forehead. "You haven't even touched your food."

"It's my tonsils," said Butter. "I think they're falling out."

Shanda squirmed in her chair, darting an anxious look at her friends around the table.

"Your what?" asked Mr. Bates.

"My tonsils," moaned Butter. "I jumped and skipped and I'm only in the first grade." Her eyes welled with tears. "I'm not gonna die, am I, Daddy?" she asked.

51

"Pass the milk," said Shanda nervously.

"Your glass is already full of milk," said Mrs. Bates.

"Well then, pass the raisin sauce." Shanda cleared her throat.

"Please pass the almond poppy seed roll," said Pam, quickly coming to Shanda's aid.

"Please pass the salt," said Susan.

"Could I have more pepper, please?" asked Gloria.

Mr. and Mrs. Bates looked around the table. "All right, girls. What's going on here?" asked Mr. Bates. "Shanda, do you know what Butter's talking about?"

"Shanda said I'd get sick and die if I jumped to her music," said Butter.

"I never actually said you'd die," said Shanda. She tried to force a smile. "It was just a joke, Dad," she said.

"It doesn't sound like a very funny joke," said Mrs. Bates. She pulled Butter onto her lap and stroked her blonde hair. "Your sister was just teasing," she said. "You can jump and skip all you want. It won't hurt your tonsils."

Butter turned her large blue eyes to Shanda. "You lied to me," she said. "You even promised and you broke it. You lied."

Shanda felt awful. Her three best friends were seeing her get in trouble with her parents. It was especially embarrassing because she knew she was wrong for lying to her sister.

"I'm sorry," she said sadly.

"Shanda, I hope you won't do that again," said Mr. Bates. "You have to remember that Butter's only six years old. She believes what you tell her."

"Shanda's in trouble. Shanda's in trouble," Butter whispered.

"Butter, we'll have none of that," said Mr. Bates sternly. He stood up. "Anyone for dessert?" he asked brightly.

"Me! Me! Me!" Voices called from around the table. Shanda was glad to have the spotlight move from her to one of her father's scrumptious desserts.

"Peach ice cream and angel food cake, coming up!" said Shanda's dad. He hurried to the kitchen.

Shanda felt better thinking of one of her father's special desserts. *She envisioned a large, spongy angel food cake the size of a swimming pool. Butter was standing on a high diving board beside the cake. Butter jumped and somersaulted through the air. At last she landed on the cake. It was so soft that Butter sunk down to the middle of it. Then she bounced and flew up into space. She landed on a distant star.*

That's it, thought Shanda, drifting back to reality. That's number twelve for my list.

#12   Bake the world's largest angel food cake. Tell your sister it's a swimming pool and teach her how to dive. She'll either sink into the cake and disappear or bounce out into space.

Four

SHANDA walked to school the next morning as usual, with Butter by her side. Butter swung a lunch box in her hand, occasionally banging it against her older sister's leg. "If you do that once more, I'm going to take it away from you," said Shanda.

Butter swung the lunch box in larger arcs and said, "If you do, then I'll tell Mommy." Butter was silent for a moment, then added, "I might tell her anyway. I'm going to tell her that you're saying mean things to me. I hope I'm not mean like you when I'm in sixth grade."

Shanda thought about grabbing Butter's lunch box and throwing it as far as she could.

The two girls entered Grayson Elementary and

went their separate ways. Shanda stood at her locker, arranging notebooks on a shelf. She felt a slap on her shoulder and turned around to see who it was.

"Hello, Shanda Panda," said a short, round-faced boy.

"Oh, hello, Dirt," said Shanda without enthusiasm. She turned back to her locker knowing that "Dirt" Darby usually only came around when he wanted to borrow something. She wondered what Dirt wanted to borrow this time.

As if Dirt's own nickname weren't bad enough, he had a habit of assigning nicknames to his classmates. Shanda had become Shanda Panda. She had wondered sometimes why Dirt didn't insist that others call him by his real name, Danny. But she was afraid that if she asked, he might tell her how he got his nickname. Shanda didn't want to know.

"Hey, Shanda Panda. Can I borrow some paper from you? I forgot and left all my stuff at home today." Dirt shoved his hands into his pockets. He looked embarrassed.

Shanda sighed and said, "Here." She handed several lined sheets of paper to him.

"Thanks," said Dirt. "I figure you owe me some paper anyway since I gave you a quarter the other day in the cafeteria." He grinned.

"Was that you?" asked Shanda, remembering the coin which had fallen into her spaghetti.

"Yup," admitted Dirt proudly. "That was me."

"Hi, Shanda." Suddenly in the crowded hallway, Paul Seckler stopped beside Shanda's locker. He looked from her to Dirt. "I was wondering if. . ."

"Hey, Paul, ol' buddy," interrupted Dirt. "Do you have an eraser I can borrow?"

"Uh. . .sure," said Paul, looking surprised. He reached into his pocket, pulling out a green eraser which he handed to Dirt. "I've got to run," he blurted, looking up at the hall clock. Then he looked back at Shanda. He started to say something to her, but didn't.

Shanda watched as Paul hurried down the hall.

Oh, no, she thought. He probably thinks Dirt and I are best friends. Gross! I wonder what he was going to ask. Oh, why didn't I say something? Anything!

The five-minute bell rang. Shanda slammed shut her locker door, and raced down the hall for Mrs. Blandon's class. She tossed her books onto her desk and slid into her seat. Leaning across the aisle, she whispered to Pam, "Do you want to spend the night this Saturday? Susan and Gloria are coming. It's my mom's birthday and Dad's trying a new recipe for crepes. They're like pancakes, but Dad puts neat stuff on them, like apple slices or chocolate." Shanda licked her lips. "Crepes are the best," she added.

"What's he putting on them this Saturday?" asked Pam.

"I don't know," Shanda admitted. "He won't tell anyone. He says since it's Mom's birthday, it's going to be a super surprise. It's some recipe he invented himself. It's going into his new dessert cookbook."

"I know. And he needs more guinea pigs, right?" Pam said laughingly.

"Well, yeah," said Shanda. "But it seemed like the perfect time for a slumber party, too."

"Sure," said Pam. "I think I can come. My parents are having people over for dinner on Saturday. I'd like to escape. You know how boring adults can be when they get together. I'm sure I can come."

"Good!" said Shanda. "Hey, I've got an idea. How about if your parents take care of Butter for the evening? When your mom drops you off at my house, she could take Butter with her." Shanda looked thoughtful. "Then maybe if your mom decides that she really likes Butter..."

"Girls!" called Mrs. Blandon.

Shanda and Pam jumped in their seats. They turned to face the stern-faced woman at the front of the room.

"Girls," continued Mrs. Blandon. "Perhaps you'd like to share your conversation with the rest of the class. Would you?"

"No, thank you," said Shanda.

Titters of laughter ran around the classroom. Shanda saw Paul Seckler turn around in his seat to look at her. She felt her face turn warm. She worried that Paul could tell she was blushing.

"Well then, Miss Bates and Miss Whaley, I suggest you keep your mouths closed for the remainder of the class." Mrs. Blandon stared grimly at Shanda for a moment. Then she began to call the roll.

Shanda went to her morning classes. She got an "A" on a math test. The math teacher, Mrs. Emerson, had written a comment at the top of the page. It said, "Well done, Shanda!" Shanda felt her bruised feelings from Mrs. Blandon's class begin to disappear.

The bell rang for lunch and Shanda joined a group of students rushing to the cafeteria. Shanda wondered what the hurry was. They all must know by now that cafeteria food is the pits! she thought. But then, the other kids probably didn't have a cookbook author for a father. The smell of canned sauerkraut met Shanda's nose as she walked into the cafeteria. She held her breath as she walked past the pans of kraut to the dessert section. The cherry cobbler looks good, Shanda thought, as she took a tray. Looking around for her friends, she found them sitting at their usual table. But another person was sitting there who shouldn't be!

Shanda's arms jerked, rattling the silverware on her tray, as she saw Butter sitting between Pam and Gloria.

"Butter, what are you doing here?" asked Shanda, approaching the table.

"I'm eating lunch," said Butter with a mouthful of sauerkraut that Pam had given her.

Shanda sighed and sat down beside Susan, across from Butter.

"Yes," she said. "I know that. What I mean is, why are you here? What's wrong? Why aren't you with your own friends?"

"I'm tired of them," said Butter. "I like your friends better."

"Well, at least the kid has good taste," said Pam with a smile.

Butter squirmed in her chair. "I hate these chairs," she said. "Ouch! There's a nail sticking out!" she yelled.

Heads turned at nearby tables to see where the noise was coming from. Shanda bowed her head over her dessert plate. She wondered what embarrassing thing Butter would do today.

"Ooowww!" howled Butter. "There's a nail poking my bottom!"

"Does your sister have some kind of problem?" asked Gloria.

Shanda raised her head to see Butter squirming and wriggling in her chair.

"Butter, stop it!" whispered Shanda.

Butter continued to squirm. Her chair tipped at a crazy angle. Pam reached out to grab it. But it was too late. Butter slid onto the floor with the chair tumbling on top of her. The sound of tearing fabric could be heard along with the shrieks of Shanda, Pam, Susan, and Gloria.

Conversation in the lunchroom stopped. All eyes turned to Butter who was climbing out from under the fallen chair.

"Look at her pants!" someone yelled. Laughter rose in the cafeteria. Shanda gasped as she saw that the back of Butter's green play pants had been ripped. A patch of green fabric hung stubbornly to a nail on the seat of the overturned chair. Butter twisted her head over her shoulder. Her underpants were white with brown teddy bears dancing in a circle over her bottom.

Butter began to cry. "Look at my teddy bears!" she sobbed. "Oh, no! Mommy will be mad at me!"

"I think I'm going to die," whispered Shanda. "Will somebody please tell me that this isn't really happening?"

"It's happening," moaned Gloria. "This is really awful. Everyone's laughing at us."

"Wake me up when it's over," said Susan, laying her head on her arms.

"Look on the bright side," said Pam. "At least her underwear didn't get ripped, too."

Butter howled with embarrassment. Tears streamed down her cheeks.

"Please don't cry," said Shanda. "Mom can sew a patch on your pants."

"But everyone's laughing at me!" sobbed Butter. "They can see my underwear!"

Shanda removed her green cardigan sweater and tied it around Butter's waist. She knotted the arms in the front. "There," she said consolingly. "Now your bottom's all covered up. No one can see."

Butter peered over her shoulder at the green flap behind her. Her crying stopped. A smile appeared. She dried her tears as she said, "That looks neat. Can I wear it to class?"

"Sure," said Shanda. "Now, please sit down and be still."

"I can't sit down," said Butter. "There's a nail on my chair."

"Give the kid a break!" called a voice from another table. Shanda wasn't sure, but it sounded like Dirt Darby.

"Everyone's looking at us," whispered Shanda. "You have to sit down."

"Okay," said Butter. "I'll sit on you." Before Shanda could stop her, Butter had climbed into her lap. Even with the offending teddy bears hidden from view, Shanda didn't feel much better. It was hard to ignore a full-sized six-year-old girl sitting on her lap.

"Can I eat your cherry cobbler?" asked Butter.

"Sure, if you promise to be quiet," said Shanda. "I can't reach it from here anyway." Shanda sat back with the weight of her sister in her lap. She was too embarrassed to say a word for the rest of lunch. She let her imagination run wild. She thought of item number thirteen for her list. It was a great daydream:

If only Butter would turn brown and shrink to a height of three inches she could go live with the teddy bears. All the teddy bears had names— Lazy, Sloppy, Clumsy. What would Butter's name be? Shanda decided on "Bratty Bear." She thought, Why does my little sister keep embarrassing me? And why does she always have to do it in front of a zillion people?

When the bell rang, Shanda lifted Butter from her lap. She led her into the crowd of students leaving the cafeteria. Shanda heard a boy's voice behind her say, "Look! There's the girl who ripped her pants."

Shanda hurried to her next class. She tried to get as far away from the cafeteria and Butter as she could. It seemed to Shanda like everyone was staring at her. Probably everyone knew that Butter was her sister. They knew that Butter was the kid in the cafeteria who couldn't even sit in a chair without ripping the back of her pants.

When the last bell of the day rang, Shanda grabbed her books. She ran out of the school and down the front steps. She waited for Butter as usual, while other students hurried past her. After several minutes, Shanda grew tired of waiting. She began to walk toward home. As she walked she thought about how nice it would be if Butter could walk home by herself. But Shanda knew that Butter was too young for that. She began to daydream.

Dad could invent a dessert recipe with magical ingredients. Butter would eat it. She'd grow a foot taller in just five minutes. Her front teeth would grow in and she'd act older. She'd be able to walk places all by herself. She'd even be able to reach the kitchen cabinet to get her own drinking glass.

"That's number fourteen for my list," Shanda said out loud.

#14 Feed your sister a magic dessert to make her grow tall quickly.

At last Shanda reached the crosswalk where she stopped to wait for Butter. This was the spot where Butter always took Shanda's hand. Their parents had a rule that Butter couldn't cross streets alone. Shanda waited impatiently.

At last she heard Butter's voice calling, "There she is!" Shanda looked around quickly to see Butter approaching. But she wasn't alone. Shanda caught her breath as she recognized Paul

Seckler walking beside her younger sister.

"Look who I found. She was crying at the bottom of the school steps," Paul said as he reached the crosswalk.

Shanda smiled at Paul. Then she noticed that Butter's nose was pink and sniffling. She couldn't think of anything to say. She also noticed that Butter's teddy bears were showing again. But Butter didn't seem to care.

"Where's my sweater?" asked Shanda.

"I forgot it," said Butter. "Don't worry, I didn't lose it." She turned to Paul. "Paul, will you hold my hand while we cross the street?"

"Sure," said Paul with a grin. He reached down, taking Butter's little hand in his.

Shanda reached to take Butter's other hand, but Butter stuck it in her pocket. "You don't have to. I'm holding hands with Paul," she said with a smile.

Shanda fell a step behind, following Paul and Butter across the street. A scruffy gray dog came from nowhere and trotted beside them. The dog

raced off, chasing a cat. Shanda watched Paul and Butter hand-in-hand. Another daydream ran through her head.

I wish that someone would cast a spell on Butter and turn her into a dog. Then Butter the Dog would run away, just like the gray, scruffy dog did.

If only that would happen, Shanda thought. Then maybe Paul and I could be alone together. He'd hold my hand instead of Butter's. I'll have to remember to add number fifteen to my list of *Ways to Dump a Sister.*

On the other side of the street, Butter asked Paul, "Will you walk all the way home with me? I like you. You're nice." Butter smiled, showing pink gums where her two front teeth used to be.

"Sure," said Paul. "I'll walk with you." He turned to Shanda and said, "You know Shanda, your sister's really sweet."

Shanda didn't say anything. What could she say? She was glad when Butter started talking.

"Mrs. Bryant taught us how to spell in school

today," she said proudly. "I can spell 'dog.' It's D—O—O uh. . .O. . .uh. . ."

"G," Paul and Shanda said together. They looked at each other and smiled shyly.

"Right," said Butter. "G. We did animals today. I can spell "dog," "cat," and "rat.""

For the rest of the walk, Butter spelled every animal word she could remember. She'd just finished spelling "dog" again when they reached the Bates' home.

"Do you want to come in for a minute?" asked Shanda.

"Sure," said Paul.

"C–A–T," announced Butter proudly.

Shanda opened the door. The scent of chocolate tickled her nose. "Dad must be working on a new dessert," she said.

"That's right," Mr. Bates said, walking from the kitchen. "It's fudge pudding cake with cherry topping. And I need a couple of guinea pigs. Any volunteers?"

"Me! Me! Me!" shouted Butter.

"Sure," said Paul. "I can't resist chocolate."

"What happened to your pants, young lady?" asked Mr. Bates as he viewed Butter's teddy bear bottom.

"I ripped them," she said. "And everyone in the whole cafeteria saw me," she added proudly.

"Well, go up and change your pants. Then you can sample the cake," said her father. "I'm trying to think of a name for it so I can add it to my dessert cookbook."

While Butter ran upstairs to change her clothes, Paul and Shanda sat together at the kitchen table. Mr. Bates cut large pieces from the freshly baked cake.

"I like coming over to your house," said Paul. "I think your dad's really neat. How does he stay so thin with all the cooking he does?"

"He has us for guinea pigs," said Shanda with a laugh. Shanda and Paul chewed a forkful of cake. It was still warm from the oven. The fudge and cherries blended together. Shanda felt that this might be the very best dessert her father had ever invented. She was proud of him.

Butter noisly slid down the bannister. Then she ran into the kitchen for a piece of cake.

"I can even spell my own name. Want to hear me?" Butter asked Paul.

"Sure," he answered.

"B–U–T–T–E–R," she spelled.

"You know, Shanda, your sister is cute. I wish I had a little brother or sister," Paul said.

Before Shanda could say anything, Butter began to spell more words for Paul. So Shanda began to daydream.

Paul had a little six-year-old brother named "Bread." Bread and Butter became great friends and spent all their time together and never bothered anyone else. They both loved to skip and hop around. They both were missing their two front teeth. Maybe they could. . .

Shanda was jolted out of her daydream when Paul stood up. He helped her clear off the table. Shanda walked with him to the front door. He put on his jacket while thanking her for the cake, and left. She returned to the kitchen. Butter was still eating. She had chocolate all over her face. Crumbs were scattered over most of the table.

"I can't wait to tell all my friends at school that I held hands with Paul!" exclaimed Butter with her mouth full.

Shanda thought to herself, I have to remember to add number sixteen to my list:

#16 Find a playmate for your sister and let them run away together.

Five

THE doorbell rang and Shanda ran to answer it. On the front porch stood Pam, Susan, and Gloria. Each girl was holding a sleeping bag under one arm and an overnight bag.

"Come on in," said Shanda. "Dad's out in the kitchen cooking. Mom's going to open her birthday presents in a minute."

"Hello, girls," called Mrs. Bates as she came down the stairs.

"Happy Birthday!" Pam and Gloria sang out.

"Here," said Susan, holding out a brightly wrapped package. "We went in together to buy you this. I hope you like it."

"Oh my!" exclaimed Marge Bates. "What a nice surprise!" She took the package and shook it by her ear. "Hmmm. I wonder what it is," she said, setting the gift on a table. "I'm getting all kinds of surprises today. Mr. Bates won't even let me in the kitchen. He wants dinner to be a surprise. He said something about a special dessert."

Shanda, Pam, and Gloria looked at each other and smiled. They knew what the surprise was.

"Mom, she's doing it again," said Shanda, pointing at the stairs. Mrs. Bates turned around to see her younger daughter sliding down the bannister, bottom first.

"Butter!" cried Mrs. Bates. "I've told you not to do that! You might hurt yourself. Get down from there, right now!"

"I'm taking the elevator," exclaimed Butter with glee. "This is the magic elevator."

"Well, get off the magic elevator *right now*," said Mrs. Bates patiently.

"You'd think she could at least behave on Mom's birthday," whispered Shanda to her friends as she led them into the living room.

"She's such a pest!"

Shanda thought of how nice it would be if there really was such a thing as a magic elevator.

Butter could get on the magic elevator. This time the magic elevator would go up and up until it burst out of the top of the house. Butter would still be on it waving to everyone beneath her as she floated off into the sunset. Higher and higher the elevator would climb, past the tree tops, past the rooftops, beyond the clouds. Farther and farther the elevator would float until it reached around the world. The elevator trip would take at least five years. Butter would be in sixth grade by the time she got back.

Shanda mentally added to her list.

#17 Send her on a long trip on a magic elevator.

"Can I open the presents now?" asked Butter. She ran to a colorful pile of packages heaped onto the coffee table. She picked up a silver box and ripped a red bow from it.

"Stop it!" yelled Shanda. "That one's from me! It's for Mom, not you!" Shanda grabbed the box from Butter and held it over her head, out of reach.

"That present's mine!" shouted Butter. "I want to open it."

Mrs. Bates sighed and said, "Maybe I'd better open the gifts now. I think all this waiting has been too much for Butter. Karl!" she called. "I'm going to open the presents now!"

Mr. Bates stuck his head out of the kitchen and said, "Okay, I'm coming. But remember, you're not allowed in the kitchen. No peeking until dinner's ready."

Mrs. Bates laughed. "Okay. I promise. I won't peek." She sat down near the packages. Mr. Bates came into the room and sat beside her.

"Here, Mom. Open mine first," said Shanda, handing her mother a silver box. "It used to have a red bow on it until a certain little monster ripped it off." She glanced sternly at Butter.

"Calling people names can cause negative

vibrations," warned Mr. Bates, patting Shanda's shoulder.

"Does tearing apart presents that don't belong to you cause negative vibrations, too?" asked Shanda.

Her father smiled. "Well, if the person doing the tearing is only six years old, then I don't think the vibrations can be too bad, can they?" he responded.

Shanda didn't say anything. She waited for her mother to open the package.

"Oh, Shanda!" exclaimed Mrs. Bates, holding up a blue woolen scarf. "How lovely! This is just what I need." She held the scarf against her cheek. "It's so nice and soft. Thank you, dear." She leaned over and gave Shanda a kiss on the cheek. Shanda glowed happily.

Mrs. Bates picked up the blue package from Susan, Pam, and Gloria. "Look, Karl," she said. "The girls brought me a gift, too. Isn't that nice?"

"How thoughtful," said Mr. Bates smiling at

Shanda's friends. "Girls," he said. "I can already feel the good vibrations coming from that gift."

"What do you mean?" asked Gloria. "I carried the box on my lap on the way over here. I didn't feel any vibrations or anything."

Shanda looked at Gloria. She wondered if Gloria was thinking that her father was a weirdo.

"Don't you know about vibrations?" asked Mr. Bates pleasantly. "Well, Gloria, my little friend, let me tell you about vibrations. They're invisible waves of happiness that come out of your heart whenever you say or do something nice for someone else."

"Are you serious?" asked Gloria, glancing at Shanda with a what-is-your-dad-talking-about look on her face.

"Sure, I'm serious," said Mr. Bates. "Whenever you act out of love, your heart fills up with so many good feelings. I call these feelings 'love vibrations.' Some of the extra love vibrations go into other peoples' hearts. Some of the vibrations travel and cover the world. See?"

Gloria shook her head. "That sounds kind of crazy," she said.

Mr. Bates smiled. "Don't worry if you don't understand it right away," he said. "Sometimes it takes a little while to start feeling the vibrations."

"Open it! Open it!" Butter interrupted, pushing the blue package toward her mother.

Shanda wanted to tell Butter to quit shouting, but she didn't. She knew she'd get a lecture from her father on bad vibrations. She was kind of glad that Butter was changing the subject. Gloria was staring at her father as if he were from the moon. Great, Shanda thought. Now Gloria will go to school on Monday and tell everyone that my father is weird because he talks about love vibrations.

Mrs. Bates pulled the blue wrapping from the package. She exclaimed with glee as she held a glass jar in her hand. "Bath crystals! Aren't they beautiful!" She unscrewed the top and sniffed. "Mmmm. Strawberry. How did you girls know that I didn't have anything like this?"

Pam grinned shyly. "We just guessed," she said.

Mrs. Bates inhaled the fruity scent again. "It smells just like fresh strawberries! Thank you so much!"

"Let me smell! Let me smell!" cried Butter. She reached for the jar, spilling some of the crystals onto the floor.

"Butter!" yelled Shanda. "Be careful!"

Butter breathed into the jar. "Wowee! Strawberries!" She set the jar on the table and pushed a package toward her mother. It was wrapped in the comic section from the newspaper. "Open mine, ple-e-e-e-ease," she implored. "I wrapped it all by myself," she added proudly."

"It looks like it," Gloria whispered to Shanda.

Mrs. Bates pulled the paper away from the box. She lifted the lid and pulled out a piece of paper. "What is it?" she asked.

"Read it!" shouted Butter. "It's a poem I wrote.

Mrs. Bates cleared her throat and began to read:

My Mom is like the rain.
I like the rain because it washes my hair.
It washes a bear.
The rain is a great big bubble.
I love you!

Shanda began to giggle. Mrs. Bates kissed Butter, saying, "That's the most beautiful poem I've ever heard. Thank you, darling."

"I wrote it all by myself, except for the spelling," said Butter. "Mrs. Bryant helped me with the spelling. But I did everything else all by myself." Butter seemed very proud of herself. "Do you like my poem better than Shanda's scarf?" she asked. Shanda's giggling turned to a frown. She waited for her mother's answer.

"I love the scarf, and I love the poem, too," said Mrs. Bates. "They're both beautiful gifts from two very special daughters."

"What did Daddy give you?" asked Butter.

"Open his gift now."

Mrs. Bates picked up a green polka-dotted package and tore the paper from it. She lifted the lid from the box. "Oh, Karl! It's really beautiful!" Mrs. Bates pulled a lacy pink nightgown from the box. A pair of soft slippers tumbled out.

"Wow!" said Shanda. "That's pretty. It looks like a movie-star nightgown."

"Can I wear it?" asked Butter.

"No, honey. I think it's a little too big for you," said Mrs. Bates. She folded the gown and laid it back in its box. "Thank you, sweetheart," she said, kissing her husband.

"And now it's time for the second part of my gift," said Mr. Bates, standing up. "Your birthday dinner is ready." He bowed from the waist. "Would you girls come and help me put it on the table?"

"Sure, Mr. Bates," said Susan.

Shanda, Pam, Gloria, and Susan followed Mr. Bates into the kitchen. He gave each of them pot holders. They carried warm platters and bowls to the dining room table.

"You can come in now," Mr. Bates called to his wife.

Marge Bates came to the table. She took a deep breath. "Oh, Karl! It smells wonderful. I didn't realize how hungry I was," she said, sitting in her chair.

"The main course is Chicken a la Karl," said Mr. Bates. "I used my own blend of herbs and spices and I squeezed fresh lemon on the chicken before I roasted it." He sliced the golden brown chicken and served everyone. "Before we eat, let's all hold hands and make a special birthday wish," he said. "That's bound to get some good vibrations flowing."

Shanda looked across the table at Gloria to see if she was making a wow-is-your-father-weird face. But Gloria was too busy spooning fresh green beans and almonds onto her plate.

Mr. Bates reached out to Susan and Pam who sat on either side of him. Shanda reached out to her mother, who reached out to Gloria. They all held hands around the table.

"Hey, wait a minute!" said Mr. Bates, gazing around the table. "Where's Butter? Butter!" he called. "Dinner's on the table. Come on!"

The kitchen door swung open and Butter came running out. "Why are you all holding hands?" she asked as she climbed into her seat next to Gloria.

"Because we're going to make a special birthday wish for your mother," he said.

"Yippee!" squealed Butter. "Can I make the first wish?"

"Sure, go ahead," her father said.

"I wish that you can have a gold dress with silver on it, and I wish I'll get a puppy for my birthday," said Butter.

Susan and Pam peeped over at Shanda and tried not to giggle.

Mr. Bates cleared his throat, looked across the table at his wife, and said, "I love you very much, and I'm glad to be here sharing your life and your birthday with you."

"Am I supposed to say something now?" asked Shanda.

"Sure," said Mr. Bates. "If you want to."

"I'm glad you're my mom, and I hope you sell tons of Misty Meadow perfume," said Shanda. "And I hope you get a raise and make lots of money," she added.

"My daughter, the little business woman," muttered Mr. Bates, with a smile.

"Happy Birthday," said Pam.

"Happy Birthday," echoed Susan and Gloria.

"Thank you all," said Mrs. Bates, dropping her hands into her lap. "I think this might be the nicest birthday I've ever had."

"Can we eat now?" asked Butter.

"Dig in," said her father.

Hands and mouths became busy as everyone sampled the tasty food before them. "Great chicken, Dad," said Shanda.

"Mmmm," said Gloria with her mouth full.

"Pass the biscuits please," said Pam. "They're really good, Mr. Bates."

Forks and knives were laid across empty plates as the meal came to an end. "I hope you saved room for dessert," said Mr. Bates. "It's a special recipe of mine."

"I can't wait to see what it is," said Mrs. Bates. "It's been such a big secret all week. What are we having?"

"Crepes!" said Shanda, not able to hold the secret inside any longer.

"That's right," said Mr. Bates. "Crepes with my own special filling. I'll bring them right out." He stood up from the table and disappeared into the kitchen, reappearing a moment later with a platter stacked with golden crepes.

"They look like rolled up pancakes," said Gloria.

"That's pretty much what they are," admitted Shanda's dad. "They're skinny pancakes rolled around a filling."

"What's the filling?" asked Marge.

"Fresh fruit," he said. "I had to go all over town to find fresh fruit. I mixed them with a cream and honey sauce. I threw in a little nutmeg, and they came out just right. Dig in before they get cold," said Mr. Bates. "I've got to go turn the oven off." He disappeared into the kitchen again. Shanda passed the platter of sweet-smelling crepes around the table.

"Wow," said Gloria, as she slipped a crepe onto her plate. "I have to admit it. These look great."

Shanda cut a piece of crepe with her fork. She was glad that Gloria was understanding how neat it was to have a father who liked to cook mysterious and tasty dishes. Shanda chewed the crepe and watched everyone else chew and swallow. The sweet taste of fruit slid down her throat as she speared another piece with her fork. Gloria's eyes began to bulge as she stuffed crepe into her mouth. Shanda felt proud of her different kind of father.

As Gloria's eyes continued to bulge, Shanda noticed that Pam's lips were beginning to twitch. Susan's eyebrows began to jump. Shanda saw that her mother's nose was wrinkling and unwrinkling. Wow! Shanda thought to herself. It's really great that everyone likes Dad's new recipe so much!

All of a sudden, Shanda's own lips began to twitch. Her own nose began to wrinkle. Her eyebrows hopped and she grabbed her throat saying, "Gross! What *is* this stuff?"

"Sh-sh-sh," warned her mother. "Dad will hear you. Don't hurt his feelings."

The kitchen door swung open and Mr. Bates returned to the dining room. "Well?" he asked. "What's the verdict?" He grinned from ear to ear, waiting for an answer.

"Mmmm. It's a very interesting flavor," said Mrs. Bates, smiling gently. "I don't think I've ever had anything quite like this."

"Neither have I," said Gloria, looking sadly at her plate.

"Mmmm. Great, Mr. B.," said Pam, smacking her lips.

Shanda noticed that it took Pam a long time to

chew and swallow. She looked around the table and saw that no one was eating very fast. Everyone was pushing their crepes around on their plates with their forks. It reminded Shanda of what dogs do with their noses when given a piece of jello. Even Butter, who usually ate anything, was poking at her crepe.

Suddenly Shanda understood as she chewed her third piece of crepe. Her brain screamed inside her head, "This is the worst, grossest, most awful stuff I've ever eaten in my whole life! This tastes like Misty Meadows perfume mixed with flea powder."

"Great!" said Mr. Bates, smiling as he sat down at the table. "I'm glad you like it. It took hours to make this stuff. I think I'm going to put the recipe in my dessert cookbook."

"This is stinky," said Butter, covering her crepe with her napkin. "This is the stinkiest stuff I ever ate."

"I think I'm going to puke," whispered Gloria. Embarrassed, she covered her mouth with her hand and hiccuped twice.

Mr. Bates smile fell into a worried frown as he looked at the wriggling, twitching faces at the table. "Come on, girls," he said. "Quit kidding around."

Shanda put another piece of crepe into her mouth and began to chew. "This is really good, Dad," she said in a determined voice. "This is the best dessert you've ever made." Shanda was determined not to disappoint her father. Gloria continued to hiccup and burp from behind her hand.

Mr. Bates chewed a forkful of crepe quickly. Shanda watched as his eyes began to bulge out in the same way that Gloria's had. He spit the half-chewed piece into his napkin and spluttered, "What the heck is this garbage? This tastes like poison!" He spit again into his napkin. "Wow! What went wrong?" He looked over at Shanda and stopped her from putting another forkful of crepe into her mouth. "Don't eat that, honey," he said. "I wouldn't feed this stuff to a dog.

Something went wrong with the recipe."

Shanda thankfully rested her fork on her plate. She drank thirstily from her water glass.

Mr. Bates looked closely at the crepe, opening it up with his knife. "It can't be the fruit," he said. "I just bought it." He scooped berries and sauce onto his spoon and tasted it. He looked around the table. "Where's Butter?" he asked. "She was here just a minute ago." Mr. Bates looked anxiously at his wife. "She might be sick," he said. "This stuff is really bad. Butter, come here!"

Butter's chair scooted away from the table as she poked her head up and over the edge.

"Butter, what are you doing under the table?" asked Mrs. Bates. "Are you sick, honey?"

Butter climbed into her chair. "Promise you won't get mad at me," she said.

Mr. Bates stared at Butter with serious eyes. "Butter, do you have something to tell us?" he asked. "Do you know something about this terrible dessert?"

"Promise you won't get mad at me," Butter repeated.

"I'm going to get really mad in about two seconds if you don't tell us what you did to these crepes," exclaimed Shanda. "Did you put poison in them?" she asked with alarm, clutching at her stomach.

"Oh, wow!" said Gloria. Her head wobbled dizzily on her neck. "Am I going to die?"

"It wasn't poison," Butter said angrily to her older sister. "It was red color." She looked sadly at her father. "I was just trying to help," she said. "I just wanted to be a cook like you. I wanted it to be extra red and pretty for Mommy's birthday." Butter's eyes began to fill with tears.

"You put 'red color' in the crepes?" asked Mr. Bates.

"I used the pretty bottle with the green top," explained Butter. "It has pretty red stuff in it. It's the one you keep by the stove, Daddy."

"Oh, gross! That's tabasco sauce!" yelled Shanda. "Butter put tabasco sauce in the crepes! I can't believe she ruined Mom's birthday."

"I need some more water," said Gloria. "I think I'm going to faint."

"Is this true?" asked Mr. Bates, looking sternly at Butter. "Did you put tabasco sauce in the fruit sauce?"

Butter began to cry. "I thought it was red color," she spluttered between sobs. "It made the dessert more pink. I was just trying to help." Butter's body shook as tears streamed down her face. Mrs. Bates rose from the table. She encircled the little girl in her arms. "It's okay, honey," she said. "We know you didn't mean to do anything wrong. Just promise Mommy and Daddy that you'll never do it again."

"That's right," said Mr. Bates gently, but firmly. "You must never, never put anything into the food when Daddy's cooking."

Shanda watched her parents in disbelief as she thought, Wow! Look at them! They're not even going to spank her for it. If I did something like that. . .they'd kill me. If I did something like that, I'd get a million lectures on negative vibrations. If I did something like that. . . .

"She's only six years old," said Mr. Bates, as if reading Shanda's thoughts. "We all need to remember that little children don't understand some things. She didn't mean to be bad. She doesn't *want* to be bad. She's just learning, that's all."

Shanda thought to herself again, hoping that her father couldn't see into her mind. "Yeah, and I'm learning, too. I'm learning that when you have a little sister who's six years old, she can make you eat a dessert with tabasco sauce in it and you're not even allowed to get mad about it. I swear, I'm probably going to go nuts if Butter doesn't quit doing things like that. I don't know why everyone always thinks she's so cute."

Shanda carried her uneaten crepe into the kitchen. She imagined Butter among trees and rivers.

Butter was going camping—alone. She hiked up

to the top of a mountain where she stopped for the night. It grew dark and the coyotes began to yip and howl. Butter slid into her sleeping bag for the night. As she slept the green material of her sleeping bag began to grow softer and change color. When Butter awoke she found that she was sleeping inside of a rolled-up crepe.

She mentally added number eighteen to her list.

But Shanda thought how awful the dessert crepes had tasted—thanks to Butter. She began a new daydream.

Butter was a student in a cooking school for little kids. All of the kids stood at their desks, stirring in their mixing bowls. From each bowl came a different, awful smell. One kid's mixture smelled like a wet dog. The smell of burned meat loaf came from the bowl of another student. There were thirty students with thirty bowls of awful smelling stuff. Then the teacher walked to the front of the class and said, "Now children, we're going to sample each other's cooking. Butter Bates, perhaps you'd like to go first. You may walk around the room and taste from each bowl."

That would serve her right, Shanda thought. Instead of everyone having to eat the gross stuff that Butter made, it would only be fair to make her taste the gross stuff that everyone else made. Shanda took a piece of paper and pen from a drawer and wrote:

#19 Get your sister to join the army. If there isn't a special group for six-year-old soldiers, start one! Make sure they clean their plates at mealtime.

Shanda returned to the dining room. She found that Gloria, Susan, and Pam had left the table. "Where'd they go?" she asked her mother anxiously.

"To the bathroom," said Mrs. Bates.

"I think Gloria's throwing up," said Butter with a giggle.

"That's not funny, young lady," said Mr. Bates to his youngest daughter. "It's not funny to see someone get sick."

"It is when Gloria does it," said Butter. "Her nose gets all red, like it's going to pop!"

Shanda carried more plates to the kitchen. The ideas came faster:

#20 Paint your sister brown and sell her to a traveling circus as THE AMAZING TEDDY BEAR GIRL! Charge people fifty cents to see her.

#21 Tie your sister onto the tail of a kite and fly her into the clouds.

#22 Send your sister to Alaska to live with the Eskimos.

#23 If you can't get your sister to move to Alaska, you move to Alaska and live with the Eskimos!

Smiling, Shanda returned to the table for more dishes. Susan, Pam, and Gloria were back from the bathroom. Gloria wiped her mouth with the back of her hand. Her nose looked large and pink as if it were going to pop.

Mr. Bates stood at the head of the table, his smile returning to his face. "Happy birthday, dear!" he said to his wife, laughing. "One thing I can say is that I've never been to a more exciting birthday dinner! Hey! What do you say we all go out for dessert? There's a great little cheesecake shop just down the road. Let's have our birthday dessert there. What do you say, girls?" he asked.

"Yippee!" squealed Butter, jumping up and down, clapping her hands. Everyone hurried to the front door, pulling on coats and jackets.

All of a sudden the night isn't a complete loss, Shanda thought as she looked at the excited faces around her. Mmmm, cheesecake. Its sweet, smooth taste would be great after hot, mouth-burning crepes. Shanda smiled to herself. It really was kind of funny when she thought about it. Who else in the whole town of Grayson had ever been served a tabasco dessert at a birthday party?

Shanda watched as her mother leaned sideways to take hold of Butter's mittened hand. Then her father put his arm around her mother's shoulders. In the clear October sky, stars stretched in a twinkling sweep. In the clear night air, Shanda watched and listened as Gloria leaned toward Pam who walked in front of her. Gloria put her mouth close to Pam's ear, whispering, "I hate cheesecake."

Six

"**B**UTTER, would you please get lost?" asked Shanda. "We're trying to have a private conversation. Can't I even have privacy in my own room?" Shanda looked at Pam, Susan, and Gloria for support. They nodded their heads sympathetically from where they sat on the edge of Shanda's bed. Butter sat cross-legged behind them, leaning closer whenever their voices sank to whispers.

"You should be nicer to me," said Butter with a toss of her blonde head. "You should be nicer 'cause I'm the star of the Halloween play at school. I'm the Wiggly Wobbly Pumpkin."

"That's all I've been hearing about for the past week," groaned Shanda to her friends. Turning back to Butter she said, "You're not the only star of the play. Almost everyone else in school is in it, too. I signed up to work the lights, so I'll be backstage the whole time."

"I'm in it, too," said Susan. "I'm going to be a witch. Hee-hee-hee," she cackled.

"But the name of the play is the *Wiggly Wobbly Pumpkin* and that's *me*, so *I'm* the star," insisted Butter.

"I think the teachers picked Butter because she's so little and cute," said Pam.

"If I hear one more person say Butter's cute, I think I'll scream," sighed Shanda. She thought of number twenty-four to add to her list. Shanda's eyes closed slightly as she daydreamed.

A kid collector came to Grayson to take all the little sisters who were blonde, six years old, and missing their two front teeth. The kid collector was a nice old lady who took the sisters to an acting school in New York. She brought them home when they reached the sixth grade. The little sisters knew how to act like normal people who didn't whine and brag about their starring roles in class plays.

"Shanda's in love with Paul." Shanda was jolted back into reality. "She wants him to be her boyfriend. But she knows Paul thinks she's a big cooty." Butter volunteered the information to Shanda's friends.

"Have you been listening in on the phone again?" asked Shanda with a sigh.

"Mmmm." Butter nodded. "I listened in on the kitchen phone."

"At least she's honest," said Pam with a smile.

"Darn it, Butter," exclaimed Shanda. "You don't need to hear everything I say." Shanda felt her neck muscles tighten as she looked at Butter's smiling face. She reminded herself that her parents had gone shopping for the afternoon, leaving instructions to watch her little sister. It just isn't fair, she thought. It just isn't right for an older sister to be stuck with a little pest all the time. Shanda opened her dresser drawer and pulled out her list of *Ways to Dump a Sister.* Her friends continued to chat as she wrote:

#25 When someone comes to the door trick-or-treating, give them your sister instead of candy.

"I don't know if I'm going trick-or-treating this year," said Pam. "My mom says it's becoming too dangerous."

"My dad said the same thing," agreed Gloria. "I've heard some very scary stories." She shivered.

Shanda looked across the room at Butter who was being quiet for the first time that afternoon. Butter's eyes stared as the girls talked.

"I remember one Halloween when I was real little," said Susan. "This guy in a monster costume kept trying to scare me. He was older than me and his mask was terrible. It had three eyes, two noses, and blue stuff coming out of the mouth. He kept chasing me around a mailbox. Boy, was I scared."

I remember one Halloween when I saw a ghost on top of Mrs. Perkins' house," said Pam. "It was really spooky. It was a cloudy night and I kept seeing this white thing jumping around on her roof."

"That's just a pretend ghost," said Shanda. "Mrs. Perkins does that every year. It's just made out of a sheet and some wires."

"Really?" asked Pam. "Wow! It looks real. It scared me to death when I was little!"

"I thought I saw a ghost once," said Gloria. "It was really weird. I was down in our basement and I looked over my shoulder and there was. . . ." Gloria suddenly leaped from the bed. She stood looking at the mattress behind her. "Hey! This bed's wet!"

Pam and Susan jumped up, wiping the back of their jeans with their hands. "Gross!" yelled Gloria, looking at Shanda. "Your sister just wet your bed!"

Butter sat goggle-eyed in the middle of a spreading puddle in the center of Shanda's bed. A trickle of tears ran down her cheeks as she sobbed, "I don't like ghosts. I'm afraid of ghosts.

You're scaring me."

Shanda crossed the room in two steps as Butter jumped off the bed. "You just wet my bed!" she yelled. "Look at that!" Shanda pointed at the damp patch on her bedspread. Then she pulled the whole spread from the bed and threw it into a corner.

Butter's sobs grew louder. "You were scaring me," she sobbed. "I'm afraid of ghosts."

"Don't be afraid," said Shanda. "There's no such thing as ghosts. Now go change your pants," she ordered. "Only babies believe in ghosts. And only babies wet their pants."

"Promise me that no ghost will get me," pleaded Butter as she walked slowly toward the bedroom door.

"I promise," said Shanda. "Don't worry. You're safe. Now go change your pants."

Butter left the room and Shanda looked apologetically at her friends. "I'm sorry, you guys," she said. "I always get stuck babysitting for her. Sometimes she seems like such a pest."

"Why don't you try to get her interested in something?" suggested Susan.

"Like what?" Shanda looked hopefully at her friend.

Susan thought for a moment. "I don't know. Maybe she could join a club at school, or join the Brownies."

"She won't be a Brownie," said Shanda. "She used to be one. But she kept throwing her beanie at the other Brownies and cried to go home. She's such a baby. I'm hoping that this Halloween play will keep her busy."

The door of Shanda's bedroom opened and Butter reentered wearing a clean, dry pair of play pants. She sat beside Shanda's friends who were now sitting on the floor.

"I feel better now," she announced. "I'm not scared anymore. But don't talk about ghosts. Let's talk about the *Wiggly Wobbly Pumpkin*. I'm the star!" Butter's face lit up with a smile. "Yes," she said, the tip of her tongue poking from the gap in her teeth. "I will be a very good pumpkin.

Daddy's helping me make a costume. It's big and round and orange. There's a hole in the top for my head."

"Butter, would you please leave us alone for a while?" asked Shanda. "We have some things we want to talk about."

"Boys?" asked Butter. "I'll bet you're going to talk about boys, aren't you? I want to stay."

"Do you want to go trick-or-treating?" asked Shanda. "I'm not going to take you unless you leave my room *right now*."

"But Daddy said you have to take me," Butter whined loudly.

"I mean it, Butter. I'm not going to take you trick-or-treating unless you leave right now."

Butter looked worried. "Okay," she said at last. "I'll leave. Promise you'll take me trick-or-treating?"

"Yes," said Shanda. "I promise. Now, please leave."

"Okay. I'll go to my room and practice being a pumpkin," announced Butter.

"Good idea," agreed Shanda. "You go practice." Butter's feet pattered quickly down the hall and into her own room. Shanda looked at her friends. "Wow!" she giggled. "Something finally worked. I can't believe it. We finally got rid of her."

Shanda smiled to herself as she pulled out her list to add number twenty-six. Her pen busily scratched across the paper.

"What's that?" asked Gloria. "What are you writing?"

"It's just a list I have of ways to escape from a pesty little sister," said Shanda. "If I can think of enough ways I'll sell my ideas to a magazine. I'll probably make a million dollars because everyone with a little sister will want a copy." Shanda finished writing.

"Now we can talk about boys." Shanda grinned.

Seven

"WE'RE awfully proud of you, honey," said Mrs. Bates. "Remember, it's just two weeks until the play, so you'll have to work hard and learn your lines. We'll help you learn them."

"Sure, honey," said Mr. Bates, ruffling the top of Butter's hair with his hand. "We'll all help you learn your part. After all, we're a family and we should all help each other." He smiled across the table at his older daughter. "Right, Shanda?"

"Pass the milk, please," said Shanda. She was determined to ignore her father's suggestion. After all, she had her own part in the play to learn. She had to know when to dim and brighten the lights. The first rehearsal was tomorrow.

"And I'll be glad to help you make your

pumpkin costume," said Mr. Bates, turning once again toward Butter. "That should be fun. We'll just get some chicken wire, glue, and orange cloth. We'll whip something up so you look just like a wiggly wobbly pumpkin. Okay?"

"Yippee!" said Butter. "Can you make it so I can wear it trick-or-treating?" she coaxed.

"When is Beggar's Night?" Mr. Bates asked.

"It's the night before the play," Mrs. Bates said. "I think it would be okay for her to wear the same pumpkin costume for both nights. Don't you?"

"Sure," said Mr. Bates. "I don't know why not." He reached out to pat Butter's head again. "We're awfully proud of you, honey," he said. "It's not every day that someone in the Bates family gets the starring role in a play."

Shanda tapped her fork against her plate. It made a steady clinking noise. She thought, Why is it that Mom and Dad always pay attention to Butter, and they never pay any attention to me? How come they think that everything Butter does is so cute, and so great? What do I have to do to get someone to pay some attention to me around here?

"Shanda, honey. Would you please stop making that noise with your fork?" asked Mrs. Bates. "It's really quite annoying. You've been doing it for five minutes." Shanda dropped her fork to her plate.

"Do you think people will want my autograph?" asked Butter happily. "Do you think that they'll give me a prize for being the best pumpkin in the whole school?"

Mr. and Mrs. Bates looked proudly at the sight of their younger daughter's eager face. "It looks like we have a budding actress on our hands," said Mr. Bates. "Who knows?"

Shanda thought, I'd really like to say something, but if I said it I'd probably get sent to my room. I'm so tired of hearing about my dumb little sister starring as a pumpkin in some dumb play.

"Well," said Mr. Bates, rising from the table.

"Now is the time for our big surprise of the night. In honor of the occasion . . . "

"I made dessert," hollered Butter. "I made it almost all by myself! Daddy let me do it."

"Are you serious?" asked Mrs. Bates, looking into her husband's face.

"Perfectly serious," said Mr. Bates with a smile. "Butter did indeed make the dessert for tonight. Don't worry. Nothing strange went into it," he said with a wink. "No tabasco sauce. I watched her while she made it."

"I made up the recipe all by myself," said Butter, running to the kitchen. She returned with a large bowl full of something brown. "I want to be a cook just like Daddy when I grow up," she announced, setting the bowl on the table. "I said he could use this recipe in his book if he wants."

Shanda wrinkled her nose at the bowl. "What is it?" she asked.

"Graham cracker pudding," announced Butter proudly.

"Oh, gross!" Shanda couldn't stop herself.

"How did you make it?" she asked.

"It was easy," Butter said, shrugging her shoulders. "I just took some graham crackers and smashed them up. Then I added water and mushed it around with a big spoon. I ate some and it's really good."

Shanda grimaced and turned imploring eyes to her father. "Do I have to eat it?" she asked.

"Just take a little bit," advised Mr. Bates. "It won't hurt you. It's the very first thing she's ever made. Let's encourage her." He spooned a blob of brown mush from the bowl onto his dessert plate. "Mmmm," he said, smacking his lips. "This looks mighty good." Butter eagerly watched him as he tasted the pudding. "Yum, yum." Her father patted his stomach.

As Shanda chewed a spoonful of graham cracker mush, she didn't say "Yum, yum." She said nothing. But she said to herself, "Why does everyone always do what Butter wants them to do? Mom and Dad are spoiling Butter rotten just because she's a pumpkin in a school play. I don't know if I can stand anymore of this."

The telephone rang and Butter ran to the kitchen to answer it. A moment later Shanda heard Butter's shrill voice call, "Shanda! It's a boy! You'd better hurry and answer it before he hangs up. I think it might be Paul!" Shanda froze in her seat at the thought of a boy calling and that he was listening to Butter's screams.

Shanda jumped up from the table, ran to the kitchen, and grabbed the phone away from her little sister. She tried to make her voice sound calm as she put the receiver close to her mouth. "Hello?" she said.

"Hi, Shanda. This is Paul." His voice was distant and Shanda felt like dying, thinking he heard Butter.

"Hi, Paul," said Shanda.

"See? I told you it was Paul," said Butter loudly. She stood beside Shanda listening intently.

"Hold on, Paul," said Shanda. She covered the receiver with her hand and whispered to her little

sister, "Go away! Right now! I really mean it."
Surprisingly, Butter obeyed her older sister and
disappeared through the swinging door.

"Hi, Paul," Shanda said again into the receiver.
She felt silly because she had already said that.
But for the moment she was shy and speechless.

"Shanda," said Paul. "There was something I
wanted to ask you the other day when I was over
at your house. But I never got a chance."

Shanda waited anxiously to hear what Paul had
to say. He paused for a moment, then continued
to speak. "I'm wondering if you'll go with me to
the Halloween carnival after the Halloween play."

Shanda caught her breath at the thought of
going to the carnival with Paul. It would be her
first date. I'll wear my blue dress with the white
lace collar, she thought.

"Can I come? I'm the star of the play."
Suddenly Butter's voice cut into the phone line.
"I'm the Wiggly Wobbly Pumpkin."

Shanda tried to control her voice as she said,
"Butter, get off of the phone. Hang up right now.

I really mean it this time."

"Okay. You big, mean, old turkey-goat," said Butter. "I didn't want to talk to you anyway." She slammed the receiver down, and Shanda was left once more, alone on the line with Paul.

"Sorry about that," Shanda apologized. "My sister is kind of weird. I'm not sure what her problem is. But whatever it is, it's serious."

"That's okay," said Paul. "She seems like a sweet kid. But, anyway, I just wanted to call and ask you about the carnival."

"Sure. I'd love to go. I'll ask my parents," said Shanda. "I'll tell you in school tomorrow. Thanks for calling."

"Okay. Bye," said Paul. Shanda heard Paul hang up the phone. She listened into the receiver at the silence on the other end. Then she said into the phone what she would have liked to say to Paul if she had had the nerve. "I think you're so cute," she whispered. "My little sister is driving me nuts. My parents are starting to drive me nuts, too. All they ever think about is

Butter. I'm beginning to think they've forgotten that I even live here. I can't wait to go to the Halloween carnival with you, Paul. I don't want to go with my stupid sister dressed up like a pumpkin."

"Paul already hung up on you," came Butter's voice again from the upstairs telephone. "To whom are you saying mean things about me? I'm going to tell Mommy."

Shanda hung up the telephone. It seemed that she couldn't escape from her sister anywhere. But at least she would still be able to meet Paul at the carnival after the play. That was one big, giant, wonderful, good thing to think about.

Shanda dialed Susan's telephone number. "Hi, Susan," said Shanda. "You'll never guess who just asked me to go to the Halloween carnival . . . Paul Seckler!"

"Wow!" exclaimed Susan. "You lucky duck! When did he ask you?"

"I'll tell you all about it at school tomorrow," said Shanda. "I can't really talk right now because Butter keeps listening in on the phone. Butter? Are you there?" she asked suspiciously. There was no reply from the upstairs phone. "I don't trust her," said Shanda. "She could be listening. I'll see you tomorrow. Okay?"

"Sure," said Susan. "Bye."

Shanda hung up the phone and left the kitchen. She found her mom, dad, and Butter gathered around the dining room table, laughing and looking at a sketch pad. Her father was saying, "Here's a drawing I've made of a pumpkin costume. I figure it should be big and round and just reach your knees so you can still walk. How does that look?"

Butter stared at the drawing. "Can I have a hat with pumpkin leaves on it?" she asked.

Mr. Bates stroked his moustache, pondering the possibility. "Why, sure," he said after a moment. "I think we can make a nice little hat for you. After all, it's not every day that we have a movie star living in the same house with us."

Butter giggled. She climbed into her father's

lap. She watched as he sketched out plans for the pumpkin costume. Mrs. Bates stood beside them. Her hand rested lightly on Butter's blonde head.

"Darn it!" Shanda muttered as she quietly climbed the stairs to her room. "She always gets her way. Maybe I should pack some clothes and run away from home. Nobody around here appreciates me. They probably wouldn't even miss me, if I left."

Shanda walked to her bedroom closet and thought about which clothes she would take if she were going to run away from home. Suddenly, her eye was caught by a blue dress with a white lace collar. She pulled it from its hanger and walked to her mirror. Holding it up in front of herself, she noticed how her curly, blonde hair seemed to shine next to the dark blue of the dress. Thoughts of running away and bratty little sisters fled from Shanda's mind. Instead, her head filled with daydreams of the Halloween carnival and Paul, who had just asked her out on her first date.

Eight

AFTER school, Shanda hurried into the auditorium for the first rehearsal of *The Wiggly Wobbly Pumpkin.* Butter was already on stage with other student actors and actresses. Mrs. Bryant stood on stage directing them. She called to Shanda, "The light switches are backstage. I left a script for you there. The script tells you when to dim the lights."

Shanda walked behind the curtains to the light switches. She was startled to find Paul standing there, script in hand. "Hi, Shanda," he said. "It looks like we'll be working the lights together. I saw your name on the sign-up sheet, so I decided to sign up, too. You don't mind, do you?"

"No," was all Shanda said. But on the inside

she hollered, "Wow! I'm with Paul! Whoopee!"

"It's really neat that your little sister got the lead part in the play," said Paul. "You must be really proud of her."

"Yeah, I am," said Shanda after a moment's thought.

Mrs. Bryant called from the stage, "All right! Everyone take your places! Let's get started. Shanda? Paul? Are you ready with the lights? When the curtain rises you need to flick the lights on and off quickly so it will look like lightning. The play begins with a storm."

Shanda and Paul flicked the light switches on and off as the curtain rose. They stood offstage, with a side view of the stage. Susan was dressed in a black witch's costume. She straddled a broom and galloped across the stage. Shanda couldn't help but giggle at the sight of her friend wearing a pointy hat and a large, green rubber nose.

Then Butter, in all her glory, waltzed onto the stage. She wasn't wearing her costume, as her father hadn't finished making it yet. But Shanda noticed that with Butter's two front teeth missing, she looked remarkably like a carved jack-o'-lantern when she opened her mouth. Butter faced the empty auditorium saying her first line. "Hi. I'm the Wiggly Wobbly Pumpkin. Happy Halloween!"

Then three little boys in skeleton costumes cried, "Help! Help! The witch is coming to get us!"

Susan cackled, "Hee-hee-hee" and raced across the stage on her broomstick.

"Don't worry," cried Butter. "I'll save you." She ran over to the skeleton boys.

From the side of the stage, Shanda watched her little sister. Butter didn't miss a cue. She did everything in just the right way. She remembered her lines and where to stand on stage. Shanda felt herself beginning to glow with pride for her sister. She thought that maybe there was hope for Butter after all.

"Your sister's all right," whispered Paul. "She

makes a pretty good pumpkin, doesn't she?" he said with a grin.

"Yeah," said Shanda. "I have to admit that she surprises me sometimes." Shanda thought about how weird it is to have a younger sister like Butter. One minute she is being a total pest, listening in on phone conversations and getting all the attention. Then the next minute she is starring in a school play and being the sort of little sister that a big sister could be really proud of. Sometimes having a sister like Butter could be fun.

As Shanda watched the rest of the rehearsal she imagined a spooky Halloween night.

Butter climbed onto the back of Susan's broomstick. Sitting curled up on top of Butter's head was a black meowing cat. Susan, with a loud, witchy laugh, flew up to the auditorium's ceiling and out one of the high windows. Butter held tightly onto the back of the broom while Susan soared away toward a huge, orange, Halloween moon.

Shanda noted to herself that this was idea number twenty-seven for her list.

When rehearsal was over Shanda said good-bye to Paul and walked home with Butter. All Butter could talk about was the play. "I was good, wasn't I?" she asked. "Did you see me when I chased the witch away? Wasn't I brave? Do you think I make a good pumpkin?"

As Shanda walked beside Butter she thought of a new idea for her list—number twenty-eight.

Butter was on stage in her pumpkin costume. All of a sudden her costume began to grow bigger and rounder. It sprouted wheels, then a door appeared on its side. Butter had turned into a coach, just like in Cinderella. Shanda walked up to the pumpkin coach and opened the door. She climbed in and sat on a red velvet seat. Then Butter's wheels began turning and Shanda was whisked off to the royal ball. She climbed down from the pumpkin coach and found that Prince Paul was waiting for her.

What a wonderful way to get rid of a sister!

Shanda glanced down at her sister who was still talking excitedly about the play. "I can't wait!" said Butter.

"It's just two weeks away," Shanda reminded her. "You did a good job today. I think you'll be the best pumpkin that Grayson Elementary has ever had."

"Do you really think so?" asked Butter happily. She slipped her little hand into her older sister's hand.

The next two weeks passed quickly. Rehearsals went well. Shanda knew exactly when to dim and brighten the lights. She and Paul had giggled and talked backstage during rehearsals. Butter did a super job as the Wiggly Wobbly Pumpkin during practice. Her father had at last finished the costume. Shanda spent the two weeks thinking about the Halloween carnival and her very first date. Shanda tried on the blue dress with the white lace collar almost every day. Each time she gazed at herself in the mirror and nodded her head in approval. It would be perfect for the carnival!

The night of the play arrived. The Bates family drove to Grayson Elementary with two very excited girls and a large pumpkin costume in the backseat. Shanda hoped that Paul wouldn't think that she was too dressed up. When they arrived her parents found some seats close to the stage. Shanda led Butter back to the dressing room. She helped her into her pumpkin costume.

"Hold your arms straight up," instructed Shanda. "It slips on over your head." The round pumpkin reached to Butter's knees and hung from straps over her shoulders. On her head she wore a little hat with green paper leaves poking out in every direction.

"Do I look like a pumpkin?" asked Butter.

"You sure do," said Shanda.

"Do I look like the best pumpkin in the world?" asked Butter.

Shanda laughed. "Yes," she said. "You're the greatest pumpkin in the world." She leaned over and gave her sister a kiss on the cheek. "That's for good luck," she said.

Mrs. Bryant rushed up, saying, "Everyone take your places. It's time to begin."

Shanda hurried over to the light switches where Paul was waiting. "You look nice," he said. "That's a pretty dress."

"Thanks." Shanda blushed.

The curtain began to rise and the chattering audience became quiet.

"Wow! Look at all those people out there!" whispered Shanda as she and Paul flicked the light switches back and forth. Shanda watched as Susan, in her witch's costume, zoomed across the stage. Then Butter came waddling out in her large pumpkin costume. The audience began to clap when they saw her. Shanda could just imagine that everyone was whispering to their neighbor, "Isn't she cute? Isn't she darling?" Shanda thought that Butter was indeed cute.

But still, she was such a pest sometimes.

Shanda began to daydream. She thought of number twenty-nine for her list.

The NASA astronauts were making a rocket launch to the moon. Butter had signed up to go with them. She had her own little room in the nose cone. While the astronauts flew the spaceship, Butter bothered them and ate their food. After a week the rocket finally reached the moon. It landed next to a huge crater. When it was time to leave the astronauts weighed Butter. They discovered that she had eaten too much food. She was too heavy to fly back to earth with them. They gave her some comic books, and some food and water. They left her to live in one of the moon's craters.

Shanda's daydream ended abruptly as she realized that there was no sound coming from the stage. She saw Butter standing paralyzed in the middle of the stage. Butter was staring at the audience. Her mouth hung open, but no words came out.

"Uh oh," said Paul.

Susan continued to race around on her broomstick, waiting for Butter to say her lines. The audience sat quietly waiting for the Wiggly Wobbly Pumpkin. Butter's chin began to tremble. Shanda knew that her sister was about to cry. Shanda cupped her hand to her mouth and loudly whispered Butter's lines, "Hi. I'm the Wiggly Wobbly Pumpkin. Happy Halloween!"

Butter turned to look at Shanda. "What?" she said in a shaky voice. "I forgot what to say. I forgot... Waaaaaaaah!"

The Wiggly Wobbly Pumpkin stood in the middle of the stage howling. Tears streamed down her face.

Shanda leaned toward Butter whispering her lines again. Laughter erupted from the audience. Shanda realized that she'd stepped out too far onto the stage. She was being watched by hundreds of eyes. Shanda jumped back behind the curtain.

Butter stood speechless on stage, staring into the murmuring audience. Her eyes were round

and frightened as tears flowed down her cheeks.

"What should I do?" Shanda asked Paul nervously. Then suddenly she knew what to do. She raced out onto the stage and folded Butter in her arms. Suddenly it didn't matter to Shanda if everyone was watching. "It's okay, Butter," she said. "Don't cry, honey." Butter sobbed and fell to the floor.

Suddenly the lights went off and the stage was bathed in darkness.

Good old Paul, Shanda thought to herself. Shanda pulled the crying pumpkin to her feet and led her off stage.

The curtain came down and Mrs. Bryant rushed out to explain to the audience that the star performer had suddenly experienced a case of stage fright. The audience clapped anyway. Mrs. Bryant explained that the play would go on without the Wiggly Wobbly Pumpkin. The carnival would still be held in the school's gym after the play.

Backstage Butter howled, "I'm a crummy

pumpkin! I'm a crummy pumpkin! I wrecked the play!"

"No, you didn't," Shanda soothed her. "You were a good pumpkin. It's okay."

Butter's sobbing stopped. "Do you really think I was okay?" she asked.

Shanda hugged her saying, "You were great. You just forgot your lines. That's all. It could happen to anyone. See? It's okay. They can still do the play."

Butter stood at the side of the stage with Shanda and Paul. She watched the other performers say their lines and go through their motions.

Shanda said, "Look, Butter. It's time for another storm. Do you want to flick the lights?"

"Can I?" asked Butter. She smiled through her drying tears.

"Sure you can," said Shanda. "Here's the switch."

Butter reached up to the switch and flicked it up and down. On the stage the lights flickered.

The skeletons and the witch pretended to be blown around by a stormy wind. Butter giggled. "I'm pretty good at this," she said. "Next time I won't be a pumpkin. I'll be the light switch person."

Karl and Marge Bates appeared backstage. "Butter! Are you all right?" they asked.

"Hi, Mommy. Hi, Daddy. I'm not the pumpkin anymore. I'm working the lights with Shanda."

Mr. Bates patted Shanda on the shoulder, saying, "That's my girl. I see you're taking care of your little sister."

"Yeah, Dad," said Shanda. "I think she was a pretty good pumpkin, don't you?"

Butter looked eagerly up at her sister. "Can I go to the carnival with you and Paul?"

Shanda glanced questioningly at Paul. He said, "Sure thing! I'd be proud to take you with us to the carnival. And of course, I want to be with your sister, too."

Shanda blushed.

"Okay, honey. I'm glad you're all right," said

Mrs. Bates. "We'll see you in the gym. Bye." She waved as they walked back to the audience.

When the play ended, the audience and student actors and actresses went to the school's gym. Shanda, Paul, and Butter joined the crowd. Around the gym were colorful booths and clusters of balloons. Pictures of full moons, black cats, and laughing ghosts covered the walls. From out of the crowd, Gloria approached Shanda. She said, "Boy! I'll bet you were embarrassed when your little sister ruined the whole play. It must be a real drag to have a sister like that."

With wide, blue eyes Butter stared up at Gloria. Her chin began to tremble.

Shanda stared back at Gloria in amazement. "My sister didn't ruin the play," said Shanda in a strong voice. "My sister was the star of the play and I think she did a super job. I'm really proud of her." Shanda reached down and held Butter's hand in hers.

"I think she did a great job, too," said Paul. He reached down, taking Butter's other hand in his.

Butter's chin stopped trembling as she looked up at Shanda and Paul.

"But how can you be proud of her when she ruined the whole play?" asked Gloria.

"Maybe you'd understand if you had a little sister," said Shanda. "I know that Butter did the very best that she could and that's good enough for me!"

"Go away, you old turkey-goat!" exclaimed Butter. "You have a big nose!"

Gloria quickly covered her nose and hurried off into the crowd.

"Let's not let Gloria ruin our time at the carnival," said Paul. "Hey! There's the magician. Let's go see some of his tricks!"

Shanda, Paul, and Butter hurried to the magician's booth. They discovered that the magician was Mr. Pledger, the fifth grade English teacher. He wore a black silk cape and a top hat. He also had a fake moustache glued to his upper lip which made Butter laugh. As soon as he saw Butter he said, "Ah ha! I need a volunteer for my amazing disappearing act. I need a little girl with blonde hair and blue eyes."

"Me! Me!" cried Butter. She ran forward and Mr. Pledger helped her step into a large box. Butter waved from the box to the crowd of people who were gathering around. Then Mr. Pledger closed the door of the box. Butter was hidden from view. He turned the box around and around. Shanda wondered if her little sister was getting dizzy on the inside.

As the box spun around, Shanda's mind wandered. She dreamed number thirty for her list.

When the magician's box opened there would be no more Butter. Butter would have disappeared. Butter would fall through a trap door and slide down a long, long tunnel until she finally emerged on the other side of the world in China.

Then, Shanda thought, I would be the only daughter in the house. I would have the complete attention of my parents. There would be no more fighting with my little sister, no more tabasco sauce in birthday desserts, no more tears when Butter was afraid of the dark.

Suddenly, it occurred to Shanda that her life would seem emptier without a younger sister. The house on Willowby Street would seem awfully quiet without her.

Shanda remembered the list she had at home, tucked away in her jewelry box. It had grown to six pages of ideas on how to dump a little sister. Suddenly the list didn't seem important anymore. She decided to throw the list away as soon as she got home from the carnival. After all, Shanda thought, my little sister isn't *that* bad, is she?

Mr. Pledger stopped the box from spinning. "Abracadabra, poof! She's gone!" exclaimed Mr. Pledger. He opened the door. Shanda stared into the empty box. She stepped forward for a closer look to make sure Butter wasn't hiding behind the box.

"As you can see, Butter Bates has disappeared!" he yelled. The crowd clapped.

"Wow," said Paul. "How did he do it?"

Shanda felt a tug on the back of her dress. She turned to find Butter grinning up at her. "Here I am," Butter said. "I didn't really disappear."

Shanda knelt down and hugged her sister. "I'm glad you didn't disappear," she said. "I'd miss you."

"How about a soda?" asked Paul. "There's an ice cream booth under the basketball net."

"Yippee!" squealed Butter. "Ice cream!"

"I take it that means yes," said Paul, grinning.

"Sure," said Shanda shyly. "I'd like a soda. That would be nice."

"Hurry up! I'll save us a place in line. You walk too slow," said Butter, racing off into the crowd.

Your little sister's a lot of fun," said Paul.

"Yeah," agreed Shanda. "I guess I'll keep her." She smiled up into Paul's eyes, then turned to follow her sister to the ice cream booth. Paul took Shanda's hand in his as they walked across the gym floor. He squeezed her fingers ever so gently, and she tried not to act surprised. But she was . . . just a little.

About the Author

As a young girl Janet Adele Bloss slept with books under her pillow. The idea was to let the characters and adventures creep into her dreaming brain at night. She admits it never worked, but it was a nice way to fall asleep.

While growing up Janet lived in Tennessee, Illinois, England, Switzerland, and Virginia. These moves provided her with ample experiences to draw upon for writing.

As early as fifth grade Janet knew she wanted to become an author. She also wanted to be a Flamenco dancer, a skater for Roller Derby, and a beach bum in California. But fortunately for her (and for her readers) it was the dream of becoming an author that came true.

In addition to writing Janet has worked as a secretary, an illustrator, a map folder, a restaurant reviewer, and a manure shoveler in a horse barn.

Janet attended Kenyon College in Gambier, Ohio, where she met her husband. They live with six cats, Toby, Maully, Alicia, Winky, Wild Jaxon, and Jazz.

"I love to dance, and listen to music (my favorites are Handel, Steve Morse, and .38 Special). I also love to camp, sing, shoot pool, swim, read, play harmonica, and talk to trees. I hate lima beans."